"Th... e. ... ... all
ass... ... ... trauma, love
an... ...hreaded unspoken through one Lewis family."
CATRIONA BLACK, *HERALD*

"Beautifully and sensitively told, by one of the great lyrical
writers of our time, D S Murray … [A] brutal reminder of
how resilient and tangled are the tentacles of tragedy."
CATHY MACDONALD

"A very special book… a poignant tale of family, love
and relationships lived out in the hardest of places."
UNDISCOVERED SCOTLAND

"A powerful book…which reveals new layers with every
reading. It is history brought to life through fiction …
moving and beautiful." SCOTS WHAY HAE

Praise for Donald S Murray's previous books

"Deeply moving." WILL SELF, *DAILY TELEGRAPH*

"He writes with an inherent understanding of Highland
culture, language and way of life." *HERALD*

"The story is told with great charm, and tinged with a
spirit of loss and yearning." PHILIP MARSDEN, *SPECTATOR*

"Donald S. Murray is one of the most accomplished and
original writers to have emerged from Lewis in modern
times, and there is stiff competition."
ROGER HUTCHINSON, *WEST HIGHLAND FREE PRESS*

"Mr Murray is a gregarious and engaging raconteur."
ECONOMIST

"O... ... ..." ..

Also by Donald S Murray

As the Women Lay Dreaming

A novel of the
Iolaire disaster

Donald S Murray

Saraband

Published by Saraband
Digital World Centre, 1 Lowry Plaza,
The Quays, Salford, M50 3UB

and

Suite 202, 98 Woodlands Road,
Glasgow, G3 6HB, Scotland
www.saraband.net

ISBN: 9781912235391
ebook: 9781912235407

The newspaper excerpts at the end of this book are reproduced by
permission of the National Library of Scotland, www.nls.uk.
The publisher is grateful to *The Stornoway Gazette* for permission to
reproduce the passage on page 225, and the passage on page 227 is
copyright of The Scotsman Publications and is being reproduced for this
purpose with their kind permission.

Printed and bound in Great Britain by Clays Ltd, Elcograf S.p.A.

3 5 7 9 10 8 6 4

To my grandson, Alasdair,
my wife, Maggie,
the people – past, present and future – of Ness,
and in memory of the late Alex Cluness

Raoir Reubadh an Iolaire

Cluinn osnaich na gaoithe!
O, cluinn oirre sèideadh!
'S ràn buairte na doimhne –
O, 's mairg tha, mo chreubhag,
Aig muir leis an oidhch' seo
Cath ri muir beucach:
Sgaoil, Iolair, *do sgiathaibh*
  'S greas lem ghràdh.

From a Gaelic song by Murdo MacFarlane, the Melbost Bard

Last night the *Iolaire* was torn

Hear the wind moaning
O, hear it blow,
hear the sea's mocking cry
come from the depths below.
The poor lads who must battle
the sea and the foam!
Spread your wings, Iolair',
  haste with my love.

Translation by Niall O'Gallagher

THE OUTER HEBRIDES AND THE BRITISH ISLES

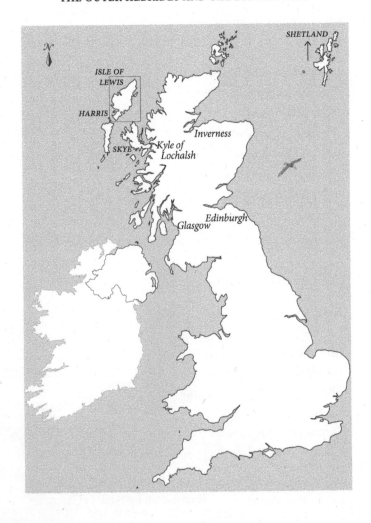

MAP OF LEWIS AND HARRIS

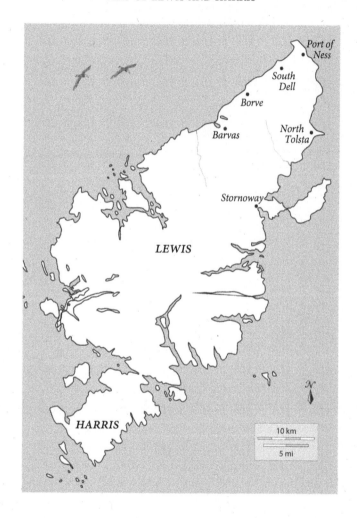

FAMILY TREE

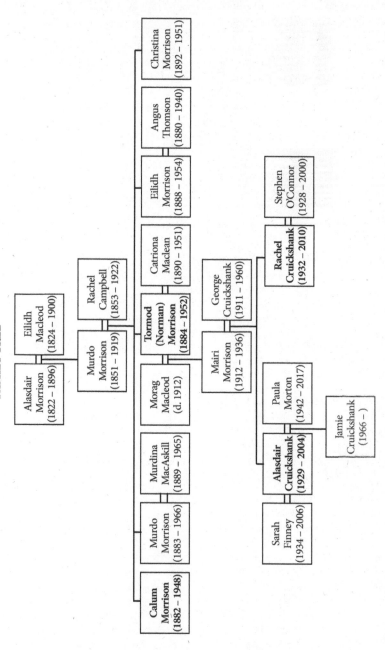

1936

My early life was an explosion of languages. Glaswegian. Doric. Gaelic. All jostling in my head. At no moment, though, was the mixture as heated as that day in Partick when my dad was caught with his fingers in an old tea caddy by Aunt Peg, the old woman blasting him in her rage. 'Hey, min! Fit div ye think ye're deein'? Tak yer han' oot o' there! Ma ain kin, a bloody thief.'

And then his response, angry and defiant. 'Ach, Ma, hit's jist twa shullins. Ah'm jist needin' tae win oot fir a wee whilie…'

Her voice sharp and loud, finger wagging and poking. 'Aye, so ye can ging doon tae 'e pub an get bleezin'. Jist like last nicht an' ivvery ither nicht! Ah'm jist scunnert wi' ye. Fit kine o' example are ye fir yer bairns? They need a da fa can look aifter him, nae een at's aye fou' an' lifts ither fowk's money.'

After that, there was a flurry of movement. Doors slamming, echoing down the tenement stairs. Dad packing our bags, turfing us from our beds in the early hours of the morning, making sandwiches, tying labels to our clothes and hurrying us down to Queen Street station where he kept yelling out in his best Scottish accent, 'Is there anyone travelling to Mallaig? Is there anyone going to Stornoway?

If so, could you let me know?' And he was also panicking a little, whispering, 'See if there's anyone around here talking in that Gaelic yer mam used to spik. See if they're heading up north.'

Somehow, someone going on that train caught a hold of his words. 'Aye. We're going in that direction. Going on the steamer to Lewis.'

And him asking the question, varying his voice all polite and sweet, as he often did to match the company. 'Would ye mind takin' these bairns along with ye? Their grandfolks will meet them on the pier in Stornoway. There'll be some siller for yer boather. Something to feed both them and you when the train stops in Crianlarich. On the steamer too.'

And then he'd tell his story: how our mother had just died a wee while before and how his sister, too, had turned ill and was not fit to look after us. ('Look sad. Look mournful,' he kept saying to us as he told that last lie – as if we could contemplate any other kind of face.) After that, there was that long journey in the train; and the generosity of those we had never met before, all that kindness they showed through places with strange, outlandish names. Ardlui. Crianlarich. Bridge of Orchy. Glenfinnan. Lochailort. Mallaig.

An explosion, too, of memories. Of a giant signal gantry. Lochs and mountains. The shunting of the front engine at Fort William. ('Come out and see this,' some stranger said. 'They don't need that other engine any more once they've hauled the train over Corrour.') The men in tweeds with angling rods and rifles. The viaduct at Glenfinnan. The couple in the carriage giving us odd sips of tea and water. 'You poor wee lambs.' The harbour at Mallaig when we arrived. The waves of sickness that swept over my sister as we sailed on the SS *Lochness*…

* * *

Their hands. That's what I remember. The breadth of his knuckles. The smell of smoke – both peat and coal – that pervaded every pore. The blue scars on the back of wrists and hands, the ones that matched the dark star on his cheek. The mat of short white hair spreading out from his wrist to his fingers. And her hands too. The way they looked chafed and rubbed almost to the bone. The pattern of her veins visible through the thinness of her skin. The manner in which they seemed always to be clasped in prayer. The tight ring she wore.

And, of course, the way he hoisted me up in his grip, almost from the instant the steamer arrived at the harbour, before I had even stepped down the gangway from the *Lochness*. I looked down at the rough cloth of the old man's jacket, noting the dark cap tightly wedged on his grey head, the black gabardine trousers he wore.

'Alasdair… You've the same name as my own grandfather,' my grandad said.

I could see my sister, Rachel, clutching our grandma's hand, her black curly hair whipped by the wind. She was shivering, partly because she had been sick on the voyage over from Mallaig, partly due to the chill of the early afternoon. I remembered how I had looked at her again and again on the steamer, fingering the label that my father had fastened to my jacket before leaving us with the people going on the boat, telling me – 'at the risk of your life' – not to take it off. The upset and upheaval seemed to have surged and rippled through her stomach, vomit spilling through her throat. One of the adults on board, a minister's wife, had tried to help her, daubing her mouth clean, holding up the long locks of her hair. She was the one who spoke to our grandma for a long time on the pier, telling her of the horrors of the voyage, how the pitch and roll of the boat had made Rachel sick.

'Wheesht. Wheesht. She'll be all right now.'

The entire scene seemed to affect my grandma, Catriona, in a different way. The heavy layers of clothing wrapped around her thin, frail frame appeared to make her shake – her long blustering skirt, thick black coat, the dark shawl wrapped around her head, all trembling in the breeze. It was as if she were a stalk of grass wavering in the wind, barely upright in the storms that life had sent to whirl around her. Occasionally she sighed. Her eyes, a shade of amber, closing. Taking in huge breathfuls of air, seeking to brace herself for the ordeal that lay ahead, the length of the journey to Ness that still stretched before us.

'*Siuthadaibh*,' the old woman said. 'Things will be all right now.'

It didn't feel that way. Not at that moment. Not after those long hours at sea, the difference between rain and waves blurring as they lashed against the portholes of that boat. Not on that pier with its salt scents and smells, the stink of oil and coal in the wind. The noises, too, were strange and alien to me. The screech of gulls. The swish of the sea on the pierhead. The rattle of cartwheels across cobblestones. Boat whistles and the clatter of chains as fish were carried between vessel and pier. (It was all such a different world from the one we had left behind in Glasgow, even though that one, too, had pitched rough and fierce since the afternoon my mother had been taken to hospital, that ratcheting cough of hers echoing in the entrance of the tenement as she was carried out on a stretcher.) Even the accents and the sound of the words people spoke as they sidled up to our grandparents were peculiar to my ears.

'Aye. I heard your news, Tormod,' one said to my grandad. 'It's a sad business that takes you to these parts.'

'It always is. I can't think of a time when good news brought me to Stornoway. The last time I was here was when I took my own girl to the pier, to see her off to Glasgow. Not realising I'd never see her again.'

'That's something a lot of people have had to do with their children over the years.'

'Aye. There's no jobs to keep them here. Little inclination either.'

A woman bent down, clucking over the two of us. 'These are the children? The poor souls.'

'That's them. But – with strength and love – they'll get over all these things eventually.'

'I've no doubt about that, but it's a long road that's ahead of you,' the minister who had been with us on the boat declared. 'I pray God will accompany you every step of the way.'

'No doubt about that,' our grandad responded. 'But as long as He gets us out of this town first, I'll be more than happy.'

He said that with feeling, looking at the Beasts of Holm, the dark spine of rock near the entrance to the harbour, and the shops and streets, the new town hall with its clock tower, the castle grounds with its tall trees shadowing the edge of the bay. He shook whatever he was thinking about from his head, bending down to lift me and Rachel onto the front seat of the gig, settling himself down beside us. Before he clicked the reins, he patted my shoulder, made sure his wife was comfortable on the other side.

'You all right? … Well, we're on our way.'

He sighed as the old grey horse trundled through the town, mouthing the names on each shopfront and pointing them out to me.

'It'll help your reading,' he explained.

There was Charles Morrison the ship's chandler, Mackenzie and MacFarlane (General Merchants) with its dried cod sparkling in the window, the British Linen Bank, the 'English' kirk they also called Martin's Memorial, the Free Kirk overlooking the harbour and the lives of everyone within the town's boundaries. 'There's the fellow who claimed one of the fellows on the *Iolaire* was trying to fiddle him,' he said, pointing out a Stornoway businessman going past. 'Nasty piece of work. He couldn't believe that one of us would have any real money in his pockets when the ship went down. As if we were fools and weren't capable of saving.' I said nothing, conscious only of the bumps on the road as we made our way along; aware, too, there was a sheen of sweat on the old man's face, making him look furtive and uncomfortable.

'We'll soon be out of it,' he declared.

'Aye. I know.'

'Leverhulme's made it a lot easier for us. Before the war,

there wasn't even a road to these parts. Now, thanks to him and his soap bubbles, we can easily slip and slide all the way home. Even take a bus if you want.' He chuckled at his own joke. 'The one good thing he brought to us. A chance to quicken our escape from the town.'

But there was one moment still to come that made him uneasy. Just out of the village of Laxdale, a man with a red flag stepped out on the road, blocking our way to the bridge that lay before us. It billowed in the wind as he walked up to us.

'Hold on there a minute. You'll have to keep a tight hold on the horse if it's the nervy kind.'

'You all right?' Grandad said, turning to me.

'Aye.'

He clambered out of his seat, standing beside the mare. His fingers soothed her neck as he bent to whisper in her ear.

'It'll be fine.'

A moment later there was an explosion – dust and stones spewing out of the quarry a short distance away, just beyond a small twist in the river. Both the horse and earth flinched and shook. So did Grandad as he climbed back up beside us, his fingers trembling as he grabbed the reins again. He paused for a moment and removed his cap to wipe his brow, allowing me to take in the full detail of his face, one that was long and heavy-boned with dark bushy eyebrows and a nose that looked as if it had been broken at one time. He had thick grey hair, swept back from his forehead, a twinkle in his grey eyes which matched that dark star on his cheek. He also had a slight twitch that was set off by moments like these.

'We'll soon be out of it,' he repeated.

If it was the town that shook him, it was the moor that terrified me most. All that desolation, that vast, empty space with the same brown shade as my grandad's leathered skin. As many scars and creases as he had wrinkles. Dark slashes of peat banks across the landscape. An occasional sheep with a straggly, shit-snagged fleece nuzzling a patch of green. A cow or two at their summer grazing, thigh-deep in bracken or heather. A dark crow crossing the desolation of the sky, its loud caw mocking our slow progress along the road. There was only one woman in sight. She wore black clothes as she made her way homewards with a creel tight and heavy upon her back. The emptiness was so unlike the world I had left – with its gantries, cranes, tall chimneys, warehouses, shops and tenements – that its strangeness terrified me. I had been taken from a world that was cosy and familiar, and now I was in wild and open landscape, startling in its difference from my own. It was then I felt tears on my cheek. Looking up at my grandad, I was surprised to see the same dampness on his own. He snorted, wiped his nose on the back of his hand, and stretched it out to wrap his arm around me.

'It'll be all right, *balach*. It'll be all right.'

It wasn't just my mother, Mairi, he was crying for that day.

Not just her with the pneumonia that had killed her in the hospital a few months before, her breath rattling and choking as she lay there in bed, gasping for air.

Not that I had seen her. In the weeks before she died, I had been kept away from her side. There was always the danger that I might catch her condition, that my life might be endangered by the touch of her fingers, the harshness of her cough. 'He's always been a little delicate,' I heard my father say once. 'It's no place for a child.'

Nor was it just our plight Grandad shed tears for, either. We were bereft and lost without our mother, and we were also dimly aware that our father wasn't coping very well now that she was gone. A broad-shouldered, red-faced man from Aberdeen, he worked in the shipyards in Govan, travelling each day on the Finnieston ferry that took him from our house in Derby Street. Every morning and evening, he would take us to and from Aunt Peg who lived in Partick, walking past Kelvingrove Art Gallery and Kelvin Hall some four times a day. On each of these journeys, he would brace himself, encountering a woman who looked more formidable than either of those structures. Her arms would be braced like a wall; her dark blue eyes the shade of the police box he also crossed on his path. Her lips would have the expressionless quality of stone as she greeted us, making it clear that she neither had the time nor the inclination to care for two children. On that first morning, we trembled hearing the question she asked standing on the front step, her voice echoing down the corridor.

'So? These are your bairns?'

She eyed up our slightness and frailty, the delicacy my father had spoken about, as if she was convinced that if she took us into her care, it would only be for a short time. It would not be long before either illness or the Devil came creeping towards us, carting us away from her door. She might be able to put up with us till then.

And then there was our father. The man who would often tiptoe in the direction of the Dolphin or the Hayburn while making his way to us after work. He would then arrive several hours later than he had said he would, his feet reeling, his voice slurring with the effects of drink. When he appeared in that condition, Aunt Peg would draw herself up to her tallest, greatest dimensions, something akin to the size and scale of the tenement block where she stayed.

'So? Whit time of nicht dae ye call this?' she would ask.

He had no answers, just a succession of mumbles and excuses, each one less clear and convincing than the last. He would then carry Rachel home, her arm curled around his neck, while I trotted beside him clutching his hand. Occasionally he would break out into song – 'Keep Right On To The End Of The Road' or 'The Bonnie Banks o' Loch Lomond', perhaps, or a chorus or two from 'MacPherson's Rant'.

> '*Sae rantingly, sae wantonly,*
> *Sae dauntingly gaed he;*
> *He play'd a tune, and danc'd it roon'*
> *Below the gallows tree...*'

But it wasn't just my father's weakness or my mother's death that my grandad wept about that day. He also grieved for his first wife, Morag, the one whose life had been taken from her shortly after my mother had been born. Gripping the reins tightly, he was thinking of her as he did so often over the years. Grandma Catriona seemed lost in her own thoughts, at a distance from all of us, even the man by her side. Despite this, I could see her attempt to crack and break the restraint that held her in its grip. She reached towards my sister, seeking – against all resistance – to draw her into warmth.

'No... No... No...' Rachel muttered, gritting her teeth, shoulders set against these two strangers who had come into her life.

After a while, she calmed down a little, but only until we reached the village of Barvas. My grandad's brother Murdo was waiting for us there. Again it was his hands I noticed as he stretched out to lift me from my seat. There was a smattering of dirt on them, a stretch and span that looked like he could grasp potatoes in the gaps between his fingers; grow them, perhaps, in the earth crammed below the edge of his nails. They looked different from those I had seen in the city, larger, more like spades or shovels, covered with a different kind of grime. None of the oily sheen I had seen on the fists of my father or all the shipyard workers who worked alongside him. A deeper, more engrained dirt, contained within his skin. It was as if swirling smoke from his years in the smithy had settled just below the surface, clouding his bloodstream yet rarely spilling out for others to glimpse or see.

I was happy enough to be carried by these hands, their lift and twirl, the tiny jig before I was placed on the ground. Rachel resisted them, shaking her head and clenching her teeth.

'No. No. No,' she said, with all the grit and defiance of a four-year-old.

And then my grandma lifted her up, grasping her and smothering all that fierce resistance with the wrap and clutch of her arm, tolerating no refusal.

I only became alarmed when my grandad walked away with the horse, unfastening the animal from the gig and leading her off with a tight hold of the reins. Old Murdo noticed this, watching the expression in my eyes.

'Don't worry,' he declared. 'He's only looking after them for the night. No better man for the job.'

'He won't be long?'

'No. He's just making sure they're watered and fed. That grey horse's quite a cantankerous beast. No one else can handle her.'

I nodded. Reassured, I grasped Murdo's fingers, following him into the small, thatched house in which he lived. There was something strong and safe about the man, his red, rosy cheeks, his bulk, as if I were receiving the warmth of a tenement fire by being in his presence. It was just as well he was like that. Especially when I stepped into the house, which had the byre within its walls, at the end of the building. It was the smell that struck me – the stink of dung from where the animals were sheltered, the acrid smell of animal urine, too, clouding and filling my nostrils, choking in my throat. Flies buzzed around in the darkness. Murdo laughed as he watched me try to swat them away.

'You're not used to the like of that in Glasgow,' he declared. 'The smells are very different there.'

'Yes,' I said. 'Very different.'

There was more of that to come. A thick broth of peat-smoke wafting over me as I stood looking around at the interior of the house. The hens up in the rafters, their eyes opening and closing in the cloud steaming from the mutton boiling above the fire. The mingling of the dampness of the thatch and the soot that had crusted over it. Even the coldness of stone in the walls and the earthenware floor below my feet. All strange and alien to a youngster used to pavements and linoleum, the dizzy heights of tenement ceilings as opposed to the cramped and low nature of a blackhouse roof.

And then came the moment I began to feel at ease – after food had been eaten and the metal plates cleaned. It was then I saw the artistry of my grandad's hands, how he used his fingers to create shadows in the light of the peatfire flame.

'Do you want to see the animals around here? You know we've got a zoo in these parts.'

'No…'

'Just look then.'

A dark menagerie began to appear on the wall, fading in and out of the glow of the tilly lamp. A fist and uplifted hand helped create the outline of a snail. Two hands flapped to fashion the silhouette of a dove or crow. A spider was framed from outstretched fingers, scuttling away into a corner of the wall. Two palms pressed together to form the shadow of a horse's head.

'Your favourite animal,' Murdo laughed, the sound echoing in the vastness of his belly.

'Aye. The finest of all beasts.'

A thumb and finger hooked to shape the profile of an angry bull, one that chased away the running legs of a man. All sorts of creatures taking shape out of the light. A turkey. A cat. His hands clamping together, the tips of his fingers showing like teeth.

'A crocodile,' Grandad said. 'I saw one or two of them in the war.'

'Where were you?'

'In Africa. And a lot of other places.'

He grimaced when he said this, shaking his head. But I didn't pay much attention to his expression or how his brother reached over to pat his shoulder. I only laughed, thinking of the old man in the jungle, cutting his way through tree creepers and branches, seeing these wild animals I had only heard about from my teacher Miss Johnstone's lips or in books.

Then he flexed his hands again, allowing one finger to dangle below the others.

'It's a nelephant!' Rachel yelled.

We all smiled after that, for all that the voice was not her own, but a shrill, comic sound. When we heard it, we believed that her time of confusion was over, that she would soon be calm and still once again, restored to her true self.

1992

It took me years to look at my grandfather's journals. For decades they remained with me, undisturbed and unopened for fear that if I ever prised open their covers, the ghosts and demons of my own childhood, their sense of loss and sorrow, would leap out and overwhelm me, emerging from the darkness of my dreams. Besides, there was always so much to get on with. The everyday business of my own existence. My work as an art teacher in a secondary school in Glasgow. The joys and travails of my own family life, one that seemed, on occasion, to follow the pattern of my grandfather's days. I, too, have had two marriages. Getting on in years now – already older than he was back then – and finding it hard to cope with the energy of my son, Jamie, I have often looked back with envy at the tolerance, patience and love my grandfather showed me. There have all too often been times when I could muster none of these, when I longed to be free of Jamie's shadow, when I wanted to escape the hold that duty and obligation had over my life.

It was, perhaps, because of all this that I put off looking at my grandfather's writing. His journals had all been created in the years after World War One and the *Iolaire* disaster in which he had been involved, each note and jotting an attempt to make sense of all that had happened at that time, a re-creation, too, of his original diaries, the ones he had lost when the ship went down in Stornoway harbour. In their rank disorder, they reminded me too much of my own life, the anarchy I felt within my own spirit: the way that one observation veers into another, perhaps mingling incidents that occurred over the distance of decades; the confusion of languages, Gaelic and English, blurring the sense of his words; even the fact that there are several events which I recall and I am sure – from my own memory – that he didn't get quite right.

There is also the disintegration of his handwriting from time to time, the scribble of his pen when ink might have been running short in the household. The same is true of his drawings. Clear and fluid when he employed his pencil in the early days, they became indistinct in the later stages of his life, ragged and faint on paper. There are times, too, when I am all too aware of the limitations of his skill. Many of the women he drew possessed the same expression as his first wife, Morag. Such as the drawings of my mother, his own daughter Mairi, someone I suspect that he – just like me – barely knew as an adult. Or, indeed, the sketches of my sister, Rachel. The black curls. Grey eyes. Dimples. They all seem to merge into one portrait, allowing Morag to age in the form of an old woman working in the peats, to become young again in the expressions of his granddaughter. All in all, it was as if, despite her death many years before, she had become immortal, gaining the gift of not only eternal youth but also continual ageing, moving back and forth over the years. And so it is with much of his work. Time reels back and forth, shifting like a shuttle in one of those Hattersley looms that used to be heard around the village for years on end. It is very hard to make sound or sense of it.

And so I set all these things from me, pushing them to the side. It is only in the last decade or so – my son at long last gone from our home and just a few years from the centenary of the one event that so marked and darkened my grandfather's life, as it did so many others living on the island – that I decided to pick up the journals again, trying to make sense of both their words and drawings. For all that it has taken me many years to do this, it seems to me important to try and provide both form and shape for the multiplicity of voices that are found within those pages, even occasionally try to fix my awareness of those years in the knowledge I have acquired since then, sometimes stepping out of my own skin and seeing the world as it might have appeared to an adult, imagining what it must have been like for him to take on the care of two children who had been bruised and damaged by their own early contact with the world, re-imagining his loss as if it were mine, narrowing my vision down till it blurred and blended with his own.

Writing down these words as if there was no distinction between us.

As if the incidents might have happened to me.

As if his every thought were my own.

Tormod's Journals

From reading his journals, it sometimes seems to me that my grandfather sought only to chronicle the landscape into which he was born back in 1884, mentioning the names of the places he grew up around, drawing little – and sometimes crude – sketches of what they looked like.

Dùn Àrnaistean, Buaile Na Crois, Na Cnipean Àrd, Loch Dìobadal, Beinn Dail, Àirigh na Glaice, Loch Mharabhat...

He wrote, for instance, about the woman whom people said haunted the little island in the middle of Loch Mharabhat, the stretch of water that lay beside the road to Galson on the village's southern edge:

It's in winter she comes to life, seeking people who will never pass that way again. And when she is aware of them – the ones leaving the parish – she calls out through the storm to draw herself a human lover. Man or woman, she doesn't care. What she wants is what she hasn't got. Warm flesh and a beating heart. Each of her lovers can only warm her for a moment before she freezes them. They'll find the person the morning afterwards, their bodies sucked of life.

After this, there is a little sketch of that island, chiaroscuro: its muddy waters, thin brown earth, a rush and stone or two. It all reveals the fascination with light and shade he often displayed in his drawings, as if, in creating them, he could escape into his own interior world, losing himself in a blur of shape and form, like the silhouettes he fashioned with his fingers to entertain us, the animals that fluttered and danced on the wall. (There was one occasion he stopped and shivered while doing this, when his hands formed the shape of a bird of prey before the light of its flame. 'It's an eagle,' Uncle Calum declared. '*An t-iolair.*' Grandad faltered for a moment before he responded with a joke.) In this, Tormod laid bare a great deal of himself, as if for all his cheer and ebullience, he was essentially a private man, hiding from his shadows whenever they loomed and bulked large in front of him.

There are drawings that show these shadows. A blurred figure introduces Dùn Àrnaistean near the beach, a place said to be an old Pictish fort where people used to shelter when they were under attack. A dark, jagged line shows the bog they called Sabhal nan Caorach, a stretch of blackness that swallowed the sheep that stepped near it every winter when they were brought onto the moor. A whirl of mist reveals the ghost that lived near Dell Farm, the one that would only be at peace when some young person died in the vicinity. I heard about this spirit time and time again from my schoolmates later in my stay. Its presence was said to stalk Druim Fraoich, haunting the stretch of road between the river at the village boundary and the nearest community of North Dell, waiting for the child it sought to turn up.

But there were other ghosts that occasionally troubled him during the post-war years. There are obsessively done drawings of the ships on which he had travelled before, during and after the conflict – the *Lochness, Aboukir, Glengarry, Iolaire*. Sometimes it is just an outline; at other times, it is a detail that captured his attention. The clan crest on the *Glengarry*. The drawings of a goat and clusters of stars on the wood panelling in the saloon of the *Iolaire*. The lettering on the bow of the *Lochness*.

Other objects or faces caught the attention of his memory. There is the sketch of a hammer with pincers lying alongside. The mere sight of them must have summoned up recollections, how he had the hammer within his grip when he raised or brought it down hard and clanging on the anvil, transforming the shape and form of the piece of metal that lay there, held in place by the pincers in his other hand. He remembered how sometimes he would pound out a horse-shoe for one of the Clydesdales in the district – the huge mare employed by Iain Macaulay, perhaps, who had the words 'General Merchant' etched out in black paint above the doorway of his shop in the village; recalling how that poor beast used to haul the cart laden with provisions to and from the town, the old man striking its rear with a stick to make it move with a little more urgency and speed.

He would draw cartwheels, too, no doubt remembering how he, his father and brother used to make and fashion them for the carts and gigs that rolled up and down the district road. He wrote the word 'felloes' alongside a dark arrow pointing in the direction of the wooden rim of the wheel, as if he were in danger of forgetting the English word for it. Sometimes the wheels might lie broken in these sketches, their spokes ready to fix and repair. It was this that was his brother Murdo's skill in the work. For one who had grown up in a treeless land, it was remarkable how he understood the grain and solidity of wood, how it needed a delicate touch so as not to break when forced or twisted. Once he was married and living away in Barvas, the hubs, spokes and felloes lay stacked and waiting for him near the smithy in South Dell, the others aware that only he could put them right and believing he would travel 'someday soon' to do this.

With his pencil in his hand, Tormod remembered how they measured thin strips of metal, bending it to fit the felloes with a roller, using the strength of their arms, the occasional touch and tap of a hammer. He recalled how they used to weld the ends together, heating it in the fire till it was white hot, then dropping it over a wheel, knocking and levering it into shape with their tools. (The tyre dog, tampers, sledge-hammer; how well he could bring to mind the nature of the work each one did, the memory of the labours they undertook with each simple tool somehow recorded both in the pull and relaxing of his muscles and the working of his brain.) He recollected how when this was down and level on the felloes, the iron circle would be cooled with water, how as soon as the expanded metal shrank, it would pull the wheel together, pressurising and holding it in place.

He brought to mind, too, how much pleasure it gave him to watch his handiwork on the wheels of a cart that rolled along the track that passed through the village, whirling round and round, more of it within him than all the travelling he had done over the last few years.

But there were other things he didn't like that much; like how he used to clean his fingers after he had helped his father working in the smithy, how he could not remove the blackness of either coal or soot, the tang of smoke that pervaded skin and cloth; how he was also powerless to heal the tiny red stars that sparks had left behind on his skin, the ones that stung and smarted, though he knew never to complain about their soreness. He remembered how on his father's forearms, even his neck and face, the wounds had turned blue, their heat and light gone and leaving shadows and imprints behind them, giving an impression of night. He recalled how there was a fantail just below one elbow, a few lesions too that used to crinkle each time he grimaced or smiled, twinkling on skin that was never entirely clean, the dark ruin of his features soiled at all times by the pigments of his trade. There were some, too, on Tormod's own face and the back of his hand after his fingers had slipped.

There was one time he had even sent a spray of sparks in the direction of the old man's face, ones which his father had only avoided at the last moment, shifting his head away.

'You nearly blinded me, you clumsy fool!'

And then that fist whirled out, lashing in his direction, leaving a different type of blue mark there. The blow would be followed by a litany of praise for his oldest brother, Calum.

'He would never do something like that. He's a careful lad when he's around here. Not a dreamer like you.'

But what was worst about his father's behaviour was not its occasional brutality, but its utter unpredictability. Tormod would watch him change his own mind again and again. Calling out his son's name, he might suddenly announce the need to go out to thin the potatoes or cut peats. A few moments later, when they were barely a few yards from the house, his father would turn on his heels, returning home again, that big, thick-shouldered man performing a sudden, inexplicable change of direction.

'We're not going out there,' the old man would declare.

'Why not?'

'I've decided it isn't a good idea.'

Tormod would sometimes repeat the question, obtaining a range of answers that depended on the old man's twists and turns of mood, which could suddenly change from a gloomy silence to unaccountable surliness in an instant.

'The weather is about to turn for the worst.'

'It might be best to clean out the byre just now.'

'There are other things to be done.'

Sometimes their whole days would be a succession of such swithering; the old man switching his attention from one idea to the next, a constant circling and avoiding of the work that needed most to be completed. Tormod would complain to his mother whenever that occurred, wondering how anyone could live in such a haphazard way. She would shrug, shaking her grey head, her thin and hollowed features as blank and impassive as ever. She would stoop as she made her way around the house, heaving the black kettle onto the hook above the fire, leaning her weight on the table as she baked scones or bread, sitting down in her chair to sigh and mutter.

Once or twice, she might even attempt a defence of his actions, make a tentative attempt to justify his stubborn, wayward nature.

'He's always been like that. Like his father before him. He gets notions. Even his own shadow would be hard-pushed to follow all that he does.'

Her grey head would shake once again.

'But it doesn't change the fact that you have to respect him. He is your father, after all.'

If this was an argument that did not always impress Tormod, it did so even less with his youngest sister, Christina. She was much more fiery than her older, more passive sister, Eilidh, who also stayed with them in their house. Christina was more inclined to show her defiance at her father's strange and arbitrary rules. Wings of fair hair escaped from her headscarf when she stood up against him, her face – even in the occasional drawing he did of her years later – growing flustered and red, her blue eyes gleaming. Tormod would watch her at moments like these with a mixture of bemusement and wonder, admiring her spirit, conscious there were times when she was in peril of going too far.

'There's a difference between respect and treating him like the Lord.'

'What do you mean?' his mother would say.

'You obey him when he's wrong. When he's being unreasonable.'

'And shouldn't I?'

'No. No one should be treated like that.'

'He's head of the household. I promised to obey him many years ago, long before you arrived among us.'

'And that means you should treat his every word like Scripture?'

'Aye...'

'More fool you then.'

She would stand rigidly then, as if the force of all the wind that ever blew across the islands was concentrating within her, ready to break free of its bonds, swelling in her a fury like the surge of seas. After a moment or two, she would walk off abruptly, going away from where her mother stood or where the other members of the family had gathered, as if she had used up her entire energy to chastise them and she had nothing left on which she could call.

'Christina,' Eilidh would mutter, her jawline firm and determined, shoulders heaving so much she looked larger and more imposing than her usual five feet or so would allow. 'Learn to be patient.'

'Just because I'm not stone like the rest of you!' Christina yelled. 'Just because I'm not rock.'

She showed this in other ways, too, like the time she stopped her chores to stand at the end of the house and watch some men home on furlough from the war working on a neighbour's croft. In the heat of the summer and the sweat of their labour, one, a fellow from a nearby village, had his shirt off as he laboured in a field of oats, fastening tight, green sheaves which stood in stooks upon the stubble. She gazed at him with a fixed and dazed expression, taking in every detail of his naked chest, the beads of perspiration glistening under the yellow disc of the sun, the brown shade of his back and shoulders, the muscles and sinews at work below the surface of his skin, even the scratches that marked his arms. Occasionally he winked in her direction, encouraging her attention. The other men laughed and chuckled, enjoying the spectacle.

'I'd like to lie down with him,' she told Eilidh.

'Christina...'

'Yes. I'd like to lie with him.' She turned towards her sister. 'You mean you'd like to be like all the women here? Cold? Alone? With so many men lost. No comfort during the night?'

'Christina...' The customary look of exasperation came to Eilidh's face, her cheeks flushing.

'Oh, Eilidh. I didn't think you were going to become a nun. I don't think our minister would approve.'

And all of a sudden, Christina was shouting in the worker's direction, revealing all her longing and loneliness.

'I'd like to lie with you! You hear me! I'd like to lie with you!'

Eilidh wanted to use her hands to shut her ears to all of this, to muffle all the words that her sister was yelling for everyone in the village to hear. Instead, however, she employed her grip to pin her arms behind her back, shuffling the young woman in the direction of the door to the house.

'Go down the croft some evening! I will meet you there!'

Even when she was brought indoors, her madness was not at an end. She threw a knife, one which was being used to peel skin from a turnip, sending it scuttling across the room. Its handle struck the back of Dileas, the family collie, before it became wedged in the wall of the wooden partition. The dog yelped, racing from its place on the floor to cower in a corner.

'Christina,' her mother declared.

Christina did not listen. Instead, she went to pick up the

26

knife from where it had been lodged in the wall, returning to chop the food she had been preparing before the episode started. She did this with the same grim rhythm with which she once gutted herring on the quay in Stornoway, nicking and cutting neatly, removing the rind from the turnip before chopping its inside for soup.

'Christina.'

Again there was silence – the brisk tapping continuing until she scraped the yellow pieces of turnip into the pot together with the salty water and small piece of flank that lay at its base. When she had finished all this, she got up and edged past the others as she made her way out the door.

'I'm going to watch him again,' she declared. 'None of you can stop me.'

And then her mother came out with a saying that came back to me years later when I tried to deal with some of the extremes of Jamie's behaviour.

'*Is tric a bha suaip-chuthaich air leanabh bhodaich,*' her mother said. 'Often an old man's child has a touch of madness in them.'

'Oooowww!'

Shortly after meeting me, Great-Uncle Calum grabbed my thigh with his left hand, giving me the most powerful horsebite I'd ever felt.

'What do you think of that then?' His face lit up with a wide smile.

'It was really, really sore.'

'Aye. Just remember that. I may only have one hand that I can use, but it's a pretty powerful one. That fist was hammered out on an anvil. Strong as a pair of pincers. Hard as steel.'

I rubbed the place he'd gripped, trying to remove the red marks on my skin. They remained there for a time, each blemish a reminder of the force and power of his hand.

'But you didn't cry. That's good. Not soft like an Aberdonian or a keelie from Glasgow. It's obvious you've got more than a fair share of Lewis blood inside you. You even look like your mother. Same shade of brown hair. Same sturdy-looking chin. And always that look of defiance. She had that on her face at all times.'

I grinned, my eyes watering at the same time. I felt especially glad that I looked more like my mother than I resembled him. There was his head, bald apart from his straggly, white sideburns, and his unevenly shaved chin. And then there was the way only half his face moved when he talked, every word squeezed from a corner of his lips, his right hand tucked away inside a jacket pocket, as useless and feeble as the other was strong. In the one time he ever spoke about this, he told me that the whole thing had occurred one day when he mocked the minister as a youngster ('I pulled a face in his direction, and the wind went and changed. I've been like this ever since.')

'Come on,' he said. 'Let's go out and see the place.'

I was glad of that. For too long, it seemed to me, I had been confined by the strangeness of the house. I felt awed by much of what I saw there at our new home, 16b South Dell: the pictures of praying hands and the gospel ship with texts printed on its sails; the black, polished range fuelled by peat that was the source of much of the house's heat; the large wooden dresser decorated by porcelain. Much of this was ornamental, souvenirs of visits to various towns on the mainland and beyond. *Welcome to Liverpool*, a plate with a portrait of the Liver Building read, a memento of my great-uncle's only one time away. *A souvenir of Portsmouth*, another declared, with a picture of a ship.

On the bottom shelf sat the Bible, black and stern. I watched my grandad open it every morning and evening, his voice becoming sonorous and slow each time he read from its pages. Beside this item of furniture was a large green hooped wooden barrel which my grandma used to both empty and fill at various times of the day, doing the latter each morning she visited the well on the croft. 'In a wee while, you'll be the one doing this,' she told me, 'so you'd better watch carefully.' I did as she asked, looking at the bubbles rising as she dipped the pail, but even as I watched, I was aware this change she mentioned would never happen, that this task would be hers for the remainder of her life. Her hands were continually drawn to liquid, hovering over it for hours throughout the day. This attraction would even apply to the fish that belonged in it. Sometimes she'd work outside on a catch she had been brought, lifting up ling and coalfish, placing fingers deep into their bellies and tearing out their guts. Seconds later, she would whirl the fish's entrails in the direction of some gulls nearby, watching as they flocked down to eat, squabbling over the food. She would rinse the fish in water before laying it down on a board, stretching it out neatly and precisely alongside the others. A few seconds later and the entire movement would be repeated, her gestures flowing as if it were all occurring in water, swimming through the air of a warm summer's day.

And then there were the meat and potatoes she used to boil above the fire; the blood she would stir every time an animal was killed, preventing the fluid coagulating and becoming thick and impenetrable; the milk she used to churn and transform into butter and cheese; the way she washed clothes that were often soiled with soot or peat, performing miracles with washboard, tongs and tub. Occasionally she even carried water to the cows who stayed beyond the small door leading to the byre. There was one there that terrified me, pitching her horns in my direction as if she intended to skewer me one day. In my dreams, I sometimes imagined her breaking loose, her black hooves trampling me.

But there were fewer terrors when I was with Calum. Even his smells brought reassurance, constantly reminding me he was by my side. There were the clouds of tobacco smoke swirling from his pipe, the reek of heather that came from his clothes. Sometimes he even captured seeds and petals from that landscape on the bottom of his trousers. Remnants of tiny purple flowers. Grains from the rough grass he sometimes limped upon. The damp reek of peat that dried on the cloth, leaving eventually a dry brown stain.

He took me through the village that morning, showing me a place that – unlike the city I had left – possessed few walls or narrow, tight confines. There were gaps between the houses. Even the new ones with their whitewashed walls and tarred roofs. Or the smaller ones – like our own – with thatch and stonework, steps that led up to the hay layered over years on the the roof. Many of them seemed to be occupied by women, who sat by windows, shifting curtains whenever people passed, or stood beside their doorways with brushes in their hands, sweeping their floor clean or hauling a creelful of peats from the stacks beside their homes. They would smile and say a few words in greeting, never letting you slip out of gaze. It was as if they saw me as the ghost of the son they would never have again, cheated out of that presence by some distant field in France, waves washing over the hulk of some ship lying in the Dogger Bank or off the coast of the Falkland isles.

'They spend most of their days trying to keep the chill from their bones,' Calum said to me once.

In contrast to their confinement, the fields behind the houses were open, green with potato stalks, lush with oats, a crop of turnips or two, their purple and yellow shades in the darkness of the earth, below the shelter of their leaves. Behind this, too, there was both the shoreline and the stretch and width of the ocean. When it was grey and dull, it seemed like its own peculiar kind of wilderness. The only shade I could distinguish in its drabness came from the waves, flapping like the tangle of sheets on the washing line behind my old home in the tenements of Glasgow. And then there were the days when the wind tousled and twisted them, when land and sea became entwined together, fastened by the knot of gales – the kind that possessed the fury and force that prevented you making your way down the village road, making you feel as if you were attempting to walk through water rather than air.

'All the way to Newfoundland. St John's. Deer Lake. Whitbourne Junction. All that emptiness between there and here,' he said, smiling as he looked towards the Atlantic.

Behind us was the dull brown of the moor. Even when it was its finest, he would twitch his stick in the direction of that emptiness, giving it a quick and hurried flourish.

'And that's where your Grandad Tormod's wife, Catriona, comes from. North Tolsta on the other side of the moor.'

'Grandma?'

'The woman you call your grandma. The replacement. The substitute.'

I gave him a puzzled look, learning soon afterwards that this was the way he always referred to her when she wasn't around, a sneer present in his voice if not his lips. However, he was soon onto another topic, his mind obviously more nimble than his step.

'It's different from the tenements you're used to in Glasgow, isn't it? I was there once in my life. On my way down to Liverpool that time. Nothing but walls there. Heck. They even seem to wall in the sky under filthy black clouds in those parts. No chance of even seeing light from above.'

The only walls that existed here seemed to be those that formed the outside of a building, sheltering people or animals within. Or surrounded a field outside one of the village shops. His walking stick poked in the direction of one, noting each layer of stone that had been built up over the years, telling me how, when people were laden with debt at a particular shop, they would try and pay it off by offering to build a section of wall for the owner.

'See that? Every rock there was paid for by some wee fellow asking for a sweet. Hope you don't ever do the likes of that.'

I said nothing.

He laughed. 'Put your hand in that pocket.'

I did as he asked, finding a clutch of what seemed to be small round pebbles inside.

'Take one out…'

Again, I obeyed him, bringing a mint from the corner of his pocket.

'And don't tell the replacement anything about it. She's pretty sour about sweets.'

It was this that won me over to him – that mixture of surliness and sweetness that was present in his every deed and gesture, as if he begrudged every act of kindness that he did. This marked him in other ways, those days when he received something good in return. He seemed to resent every time someone stretched out a hand to help him too. I would see him glare if, say, a neighbour tore a piece of oatmeal bread to give him, bristling as if it were an insult to his infirmity, a sign that he was unable to perform the simplest task. I saw this look too once when he slipped on the moor where we had gone to look for sheep. His walking stick lashed in my direction when I tried to give a hand.

'Away with you!' he snarled.

And then I watched as he used that stick to haul himself to his feet, inching up on its height, which was fixed into the earth; making sure he gained his balance again, that he was rooted in the moor.

'There! There! I've got you!' he announced.

He grinned in my direction.

'I like to do it for myself,' he said.

It was, perhaps, because of this sense of independence that I liked to spend as much time with him out as I could, learning the ways and wonders of the moor. It was not drab and dull, the way it had seemed when I had first seen it. Flags of bog-cotton grass would add light and brightness to its shadows. Green bracken. The turns and twists of heather. The tiny yellow flowers that glinted among the toughness of their stalks. The lark's song could be heard sometimes when we walked, echoing across streams which disappeared under layers of green in what people called peat-pipes, which criss-crossed the bogs. He'd wave his stick and point out a snipe with its wings drumming overhead, the green-blue shades of a lapwing with its loud persistent cry. And, of course, sheep gained his attention. He might hook one that lay swamped within a bog, its fleece green, eyes and tongue picked out by the beaks of gulls or crows, perhaps, even the bones of its skeleton poking outwards, its flesh long laid bare. He'd note the pattern of marks cut out on a sheep's ears, recognising who it belonged to through this array of small notches and tears.

'I'll go and tell them when I get home,' he'd say.

There was one day when he showed me how to make a *toll-braim* or 'fart-hole'. He poked the tip of his walking stick into the blackness of a bog, listening to it bubble and belch as he did so, his giggle nearly as loud as mine. And then there would be these rare moments when he'd admit his vulnerability and accept my help, aware that my life and energy allowed me to do things he might not be able to do.

'Go and check that nest over there. There's probably a couple of eggs in it.'

'See if you can catch that bird!'

I would do what I could, slipping a clutch of lapwing eggs inside my pocket, capturing some wounded snipe I had trapped. There was a gosling, too, I found, calling out in search of its mother. His one good hand accepted all this gratefully. He'd smile at my gifts, sit on a stone or slope for a while and start telling one of his stories. Sometimes these were about what other men had told him of their lives, like Lachie Mor in the neighbouring village of North Dell who had spent a few years in Canada. He would recount their experiences as though they were his own, as if in some alternative existence, he had not been crippled and confined by the weaknesses of his own body.

'It's a good life here. Much better than starving in other places. That's what the likes of Lachie Mor would have done if he'd stayed in Canada. Always God's plenty here if you know where to look.'

He spoke to me about how Lachie and his wife, Oighrig, had voyaged there, how they had slipped away together on the *Metagama*, travelling across the sea to St John's. When they arrived, Lachie and Oighrig had walked holding hands for the first time, clutching one another's fingers as tightly as limpets clung onto rock, as if the icy winds of Newfoundland could blow them away from each other's sides, never to make contact again.

'They walked down a place called Water Street,' Calum said, smiling in wonder, the detail in his story such that it seemed as though he could recall the tall ships in the harbour, with either their sails flapping or a long furl of smoke puffing from chimneys. All around them was a tight mingling of smells, each one catching them unawares. The oil from boats with cargoes of coal and timber. The tang of salt fish and local tanneries. The unfamiliar, heady scent of a brewery. As they wandered round, the smells coiled around their bodies, close as the ropes that curled round giant spokes in the ropework factories, seeping into clothing and skin.

'And that wasn't the worst of it,' Calum declared, his eyes gleaming as he spoke of the experience of others, telling of how Lachie and Oighrig had travelled elsewhere, still clutching hands, only prising away from each other those times when they were forced to do so – like when they signed on to provide labour for a farm in Ontario. The names of strange places whirled past them on their journey in its direction.

'I keep hearing Lachie talking of them. Whitbourne Junction. Badger. Deer Lake. Stephenville Crossing...'

Each one was as exotic and alien as the landscape where their location was found. Most unnerving of all – according to Calum – were the acres of empty desolation men called the Gaff Topsails. They gaped through the train carriage window at how barren and bleak it all appeared. They tried to imagine living on it, how the cold blade of the wind must shape and sculpt human skin in the same way as it did rock, exposing the bone that lay beneath the surface.

'Worse than any of the moors here, Alasdair. Much worse than them.'

And then there was that farmland where the wind seemed to be all that a man could swallow in the winter, gulping it down to fill his throat. In that season, there was the endless snow. In spring, the grip of a hoe in his fingers, hacking endlessly at the earth. There was the sound of both his own name and that of Oighrig – 'Lachlan and Erica' – on the farmer's lips. They both sounded like curses when they were called out, echoing over field and kitchen. It was this that forced them to slip across the border to the States when the chance arrived, finding work in a factory in Detroit. They were only there a short time when their lives shifted and altered once more.

'The factories were paying folk off, Alasdair. And Oighrig had a baby on the way.'

He shook his head, scratching some lichen off the rock where he was sitting with his thumbnail.

'Poor souls. They had no choice but to go home. To the land of sad spinsters and widows, where the only men are bitter old souls like me.'

He'd haul himself up, straining to his feet with the

help of his walking stick. The effort seemed all the greater with the recognition that he, too, had no choice about his destination.

He had to – eventually – go home too.

Tormod's Journals

There are some pages in my grandfather's journals where there isn't much written about people. Far more about horses. There are drawings of heads and outlines, barrel chests, thick manes, the height of their withers, powerful hindquarters, turned-up hooves, ears sharp as the tips of knives, cannon, fetlock, croup, each etched out in astonishing detail. Some are seal-brown, ash-grey, a muddy shade of white. Sometimes, there are drawings of horse-bones – a skull, the atlas bone that allows the horse to shift its head from side to side, a collection of vertebrae that make up the animal's spine. There is a list too of all the words for 'horse' he had encountered in various languages.

Each. Equus. Capall. Ceffyl. Cheval. Pferd. Caballo.

Alongside, a record of some of the other words he had heard that were connected to the animal.

Kelpie. Each-uisge. Unicorn. Pegasus. The Trojan Horse. Buraq.

The last was a word he'd heard from a lascar from India with whom he had worked on the *Glengarry*. One responsible for loading shells if the vessel was ever attacked. The man had told him it was the name of the steed that carried the prophets to heaven. Given the nature of his work, it seemed an appropriate word for him to come out with. A slip of his fingers and he would be on his way.

My grandfather's creations ranged in shape from the might of the Clydesdale to the cross-bred ponies most of the people possessed to take their peats home and plough their land: skinny, scrawny creatures, for the most part, with barely enough grazings for them to feast upon. There are also Eriskay, Highland and Shetland ponies, even the racehorse he had glimpsed one day on the pier at Liverpool, being put on to a ship bound for Ireland.

A wonderful moment, he wrote, wistfully. *Something I'll never forget.*

It is clear that these fabulous creatures were as much myth as the one he had magicked on the wall that first evening we were together, the time when Rachel did that rare thing – spoke a word that was neither 'yes' or 'no' in the first few months after our mother's death.

I recall him once sitting at our dinner table talking about that long silence and how she might be cured of it. It was typical of my grandfather that he even spoke about that by way of mentioning horses, his every word a reminder of how much he loved the animal, how he was most at ease when he had one – even a neighbour's, taken to his smithy to be shod – by his side.

'You know how I manage to tame a wild one, how I quieten down one that's wild or restless or spooked?'

Both Calum and Grandma looked at him, wondering what he was about to say next.

'I let her run around for a wee while, keeping an eye on her and making myself as big as I can be. After that, I watch for signs. How she might cock an ear in my direction, lick and chew. How wide her eyes are. The narrower they are, the more she is at ease, the less suspicious she is of the world. Finally, she lowers her head, looking in my direction. When I see that, I just turn and walk away, knowing she will soon be following in my footsteps, trotting along behind me.'

'You think that wee girl can be tamed, that she's like a horse?' Calum muttered.

'She is in some ways. The way she wanders round the village in a dream, sniffing which direction she should go. She's also as dumb and speechless as one at the moment. The only time she makes a sound, she puts on a funny voice, as if she's a sheep or a hen.'

'Well, I've never seen a horse doing these kinds of things,' Calum snorted.

'Oh, that's not true. Remember the racehorse old Shonnie got by mistake from the mainland? The one he called Flamenco?'

'Aye, she ran around this place for weeks after she came here. Utterly wild,' Calum said, laughing at the memory of the horse with the ridiculous name. 'One minute she'd be out on the moorland. The next, near the shore, heading towards the beach and Dùn Àrnaistean. It took us weeks to catch her. And even when we did, she was back doing the same again the following week. After a time, we didn't bother looking for her again.' Calum tapped his good hand on the table. 'Well, this wee lass is just like that. Same wild spirit as Flamenco.'

'That's only because Shonnie didn't have the skill or patience for her,' Grandad said. 'A lot can be done if you can take your time and wait.'

Calum shook his head, rising from his seat. 'Skill and patience, my arse. Some creatures are just made that way. Boy, girl and horse.'

A few moments later and he was out the door once more, heading out into the whip and lash of rain. He left a whirl of words behind him, echoing in the silence of our home.

'You'd think that this family would learn. There's some things you just can't wait for. Some things you just can't tolerate. We waited for a long time for Christina to get better – and there was no improvement there!'

Grandad said nothing in response to that, their sister only spoken about in whispers in our home. She had been taken away in a straitjacket to the lunatic asylum in Inverness some time during the war, her fits and rages too difficult and unpredictable for the family to handle. As a boy, I heard about her through hints and whispers, but I discovered more in the journals. There was the time she tried to throw boiling water at her father, missing him by inches with the splash. There was the other occasion she had attempted to stab him with the edge of a spade. And then there were the times she had turned her anger on herself, when she had run in the direction of the cliffs on the edge of the village, near Dùn Àrnaistean, determined to put an end to her life. These were days that were barely remembered in 1936, disappearing in a fog that was as black and forbidding as the nature of her supposed failings and frailties.

Yet even if she was hardly ever mentioned, she was a continual presence in our house. Those who recalled her presence – like my grandmother and great-uncle – saw faint traces of her in Rachel's inexplicable silence, the way she would go for long walks on her own, as if the ghost of her great-aunt's madness was once again visiting our house, even if it was in a different form and shape. It was only my grandfather who dismissed that thought, grimacing when even a suspicion of the idea would cross anyone else's lips.

'She's just a wee girl. Hushed by grief. There's nothing else to it. Nothing else at all.'

The truth is, however, that my grandfather was like few men I have ever met – skilled in watching and waiting. It is apparent in his drawings, with all their skill and close observation. Every shift and stirring of a horse's mane. The way their eyes widen and narrow, taking in the wholeness of their world. Every detail noted of hoof or tail. He would draw them, too, as they looked when they drew a cart full of hay behind them or a load of peats. It is as if he were inhaling them, in much the same way as he sucked in the tobacco from the pipe that was – like most of the men on the island – an almost constant presence in his mouth; allowing their movement to become part of his breath, the rhythm of his chest, mimicking the beat of his pulse.

Most of all, though, that same patience was present in the way he tolerated his life as a blacksmith. It was not what he had set out or wanted to be – that life had been chosen for him when his brother Calum had lost his inheritance through an unknown fever crippling him while he waited for his vessel in Birkenhead a week or two after the beginning of the Great

War, on that journey that had taken him through my home city of Glasgow. It was said that the illness had occurred after he had slept the night in wet blankets, cocooned within them and on a damp matress. When he woke in the morning, he was unable to move a muscle on the right side of his body. Even his lips and eyelids could barely twitch. Later, arriving on the pier at Stornoway, the sailors had tried to carry Calum down the gangway from the deck of the *Sheila* on a stretcher. He yelled and shouted, determined to go down on his own.

'You think I'm a bloody invalid? What makes you think I need your bloody arm to cling on to?'

The illness meant an end to the division of labour between the two brothers. Before the war, it was Calum who had followed their father's trade, the one who had mastered the bellows and anvil, the hammer and forge. He was the one who had been at ease in its heat and blackness. His younger brother even did the occasional sketch in his journals which showed Calum in his shirtsleeves and leather apron, drumming and straightening a sheet of metal stretched out before him, looking as if he belonged in that place. In contrast, Tormod was ill-at-ease among sparks and cinders, sweat and grime. Each time they were in close proximity, they left, courtesy of his clumsiness, scars and small marks on his skin. This resulted in the moment when his father had snarled at him when he was pounding a nail into a stretch of wood.

'You're throttling that hammer, failing to put it in straight.'

He snatched it away from his son's fingers.

'Hold it further down the handle. Now hit it, hit the nail upon the head. There's a beat to it. A ring and a rhythm. If you listen, you'll know you've hit it right, by the sound.'

But Tormod was deaf to that kind of music, only beginning to hear it after he had practised for hours on hours. Whereas, with horses, he could pick up the slightest note, the smallest change in the rhythm of their breathing, the opening and closing of their eyes, or the way their hooves clipped across the ground. He could tell the nature of the illness they were suffering.

'That's your art,' his father said one day, grinning. 'That's your skill and you'd be best off sticking to it.'

There were reasons why he could not follow his father's advice. Not only was there Calum's illness and his sister Christina's madness, how for a long time there always had to be someone keeping an eye on her around the house, aware that at any moment one of these spits of rage and fury might come. Perhaps, too, there was his grief at the loss of the woman he loved more than any other – Morag, my mother's mother and my true grandmother. Her passing took away much of his zest for life, his pleasure even in working with horses. Yet this last sorrow is only noted in the journals with restraint and reticence, as if he was terrified that his feelings might overwhelm him, that his sadness at her absence might sweep him away. It is for this reason that there is very little written about her, only that they were playmates together.

We often ran errands together, when someone's cow could not be milked, we took some to their house.

Beside this, a blur of legs and arms, as if he was trying to see her once again but the passage of years made it impossible for him. It is only when she is an adult that we actually 'see' her for the first time. Outlined in these portraits, we can see a proud, beautiful woman, all dark curls and quiet intense gaze, her body strong and curvaceous. There is one where her head is mainly hidden below a shawl. A shy smile slips from her face; her eyes sparkle, bright and flirtatious. There is another where her arm is curled round the indistinct outline of a child. Clearly, this is the memory of one she posed for, holding my mother as a baby, a record of her birth, a woman I can barely remember. I feel my eyes well up every time I see her, aware that this is only a few weeks before Morag passed away. I am still puzzled about the reasons for this. The only answer I ever obtained was from Calum one time we were out together on the moor.

'Some woman's problems,' he grunted. 'But don't ask me what they were. I'm not exactly an expert about things like that. I had no great need of the knowledge.'

He walked away after that, his attention suddenly caught by a buzzard landing on a tussock a short distance away.

'*Clamhan!*' he shouted. '*Clamhan cac!*'

As I look at these pictures as an adult, it occurs to me that there is more than a little idealisation of her features – that in their mixture of the maternal and the erotic, these images seem just too perfect. Once when I was in his home, I discovered a drawing he had sketched of her within the pages of one of the journals. Unfolding it, I had seen a young woman with features that were not unlike my own sister's – black curly hair, pale grey eyes the shade of the Atlantic Ocean on a dull and overcast day, a dimple in one of her rounded cheeks. Alongside it, there was a loop of hair, tied and fastened by a few strands. At one time, it had clearly been a raven shade of black, but over the years, it had lost a little of its lustre and shade, just as it would have done if Morag had lived. I wonder if my grandfather's fingers had helped to wear its colours away, as he wound it in his touch the occasional evening in his home or, perhaps, during the time he was in the Naval Reserve during the war.

Even back then, I'd wondered how his second wife, Catriona – the woman I always saw as my grandmother – thought about these writings, this memento of his life with another, one who would always possess the perfection of youth. They must have been hard for her to live with, knowing that whatever she did in this life, she would always be second best, 'the replacement', 'the substitute', as Calum might say. This was especially true because of the contrast in their features. The first wife, Morag, young, strong, ardent, my grandfather's passion for her evident in the way he wanted to record her features. Even when he was an old man, he must have sat there dreaming of her, recalling her in a succession of hues and moods, the different seasons of her short life etched out by him on the page – from the blur and energy of her teenage years to the quiet serenity that can be seen when she holds and clutches their child; picturing, too, her body as she lay stretched out naked before him, her arm curled behind her head, him feasting his eyes upon her. It is easy to imagine his need and longing for her touch, the still nights when they must have slipped out from their house to go to the shoreline, that thirst for one another that prevailed back then.

There is none of that in his portrayals of Grandma Catriona. She is seen only in outline and in the distance, a thin, tall shadow of a woman, her head almost as if it were on top of a stick, in essence the same person as the one who met us at the pier that day, a stern bun upon her head, pursed lips, a shawl upon her narrow shoulders. Again, there is the same passivity in her face and manner as there was when she greeted us the moment the *Lochness* arrived, as if she was reluctant to reach down and hold us, even though she was probably well aware that this was what people were meant to do on such occasions, trying to assuage the grief of children and make it disappear.

It has taken me a long time to see through her rigidity, the way her hands seemed only to clasp in these long prayers she used to utter all the time, and to recognise that she, too, was fractured and broken. A decade or two later, Murdo told me the reason why, sitting at the fireside in his home in Barvas.

'You know it was her second marriage too?'

'No. I didn't.'

'Aye. She even had a son. A fellow called Donald.' He probed the fire with a poker, stoking up the flames. 'Her first husband was a man called William Gunn, who lived in North Tolsta. A fisherman. I was there when his body was brought to the pier in Stornoway. He got caught in the nets.'

'And then she married my grandad?'

'It wasn't that unusual at the time. She was on her own. Her husband's family was willing to look after the boy. They had no need of her. In fact, she was just an obstacle to her husband's brother getting the croft. And your grandfather needed a mother to bring up his daughter, Mairi. So an arrangement was made.'

'And Grandad accepted this?'

Murdo sighed. 'I don't think he even thought for two

minutes about it. Our mother brought the news to him. We were all around him at the time, while she explained about the widow woman across the moor and how her people had suggested that she might marry him. All I can remember is the way he bowed his head, looking at his fingers, knowing that the love of his life was gone and he would have to look to doing the best for the child.'

'And? What did he say?'

'If it is your will, I'll do it…'

'Oh.'

'And a moment or two later, Calum, who was dead against this choice, turned on him and yelled, "You don't allow other people to choose your marriage partners. Not after all you had. A man needs more than that to keep the chill from his bones."'

1936

There are other illustrations in the journals, small reminders of the many ways Grandad had of making hand-shadows. Fingers splayed above a bird-like shape became a lapwing's crest, Grandad's lips mimicking its cry. A hand stretched out was transformed into the antlers of a stag. A ball of wool perched on a fingertip helped to become the outline of a young woman in her nightgown. Two hands laid on top of one another shaping a pig. The journals even contain recollections of that time he was performing this game when Shonnie, the old postman, arrived with a letter, a gust of laughter escaping from him.

'There's no fool like an old fool. What on earth are you up to today?' he grinned.

'Wait and see…'

Moments later and the envelope was used to create a bow-tie for a blunt-faced man. An instant afterwards and it became a top-hat for a gentleman, his expression changing all the time. One instant, serious and stern; the next, mocking and laughing.

'Where did you learn all of these?' Shonnie asked.

'I got them in a book I came across once. That's why this fellow has to listen to his teacher when he goes to school on Monday. He'll learn a lot more if he does.'

And then, as soon as Shonnie left, he put on his spectacles, straining to read the address that was scribbled upon it.

'It's from your dad,' he told us.

Using his thumb, he opened it, taking out a thin blue sheet to read the words, his voice slow and stumbling in the weak blaze of the fire.

'Dear Alasdair and Rachel.
I am writing you this letter as I know it'll be your first
day in Cross school soon. It'll be strange for the two
of you. In Alasdair's case, it will be very unlike his old
school. Not so big and unfriendly. For you, Rachel, the
whole thing will be new. Try not to be frightened by
it. You'll soon get used to it. All the sums and English
words. After a wee while, you won't be able to think
about anything else. Be nice to your Granny and
Grandad and make sure you look after them. They're
really good to look after you. Much better than spending
the evenings with your aunt. Your mother used to tell
me about all the laughs she had with your Grandad
when she was young. Nothing will have changed as far
as that goes...'

I chuckled, remembering how it had been when she was alive and in our home. I recalled my mother's laughter, the way she would sometimes talk about her father and his energy and vitality when he was with them, enjoying the company of children. Moments later, she would sigh and become wistful. ('Of course, you'll probably never meet him. He lives so far away. But I wish you would. I wish you would.')

Rachel's eyes just gleamed, staring in the direction where the hand-shadows had been, as if her silence was attempting to will and summon them back. Grandad looked towards her, shaking his head as he did so often in her company, wondering how to conjure her out of her quiet.

'You're lucky children. You have a dad who loves you,' he said.

'I know,' I answered.

'It's just that it's hard for some men. The looking-after of children. The loss of a wife. That's why he acts the way he does sometimes.'

Grandma looked at him with pursed lips, as if she wanted to say something about the matter, but couldn't. Not when we were present. Grandad glanced away from her, shaking his head.

'I'll tell you what we'll do. Just to celebrate you going back to school. We'll have a chicken for dinner on Sunday. Think that's a good idea?'

I looked over at Rachel, waiting for her to answer. She seemed to be entranced by the light of the peat fire, another reason for not saying a word.

'What do you think, Rachel?' I asked.

Eventually, she nodded.

'Great!' I said. 'That would be lovely.'

'Good. We'll get that ready then. I have my own special way of preparing for the feast.'

'What's that?' I asked.

'This.' Grandad did something which he claimed helped him get ready for the feast, imitating the posture and noise of a hen. He hefted up his shoulders, making his way daintily around the room. '*Buk – buk – buk – buk – bacagh – buk – buk – bacagh – buk – buk – buk – buk – buk – buk – buk – bacagh …*'

'The man's mad.' Grandma pursed her lips again. 'The man's mad.'

'*Buk – buk – buk – buk – bacagh,*' Grandad squawked again.

Yet for all the gusto of his performance, there was no sign of Grandad when that meal had to be prepared. He stepped out of the house, heading towards the shoreline, seeking – or so he said – to make sure that the oats were still green, the stalks of potatoes still strong and vigorous above the surface. Shortly after his disappearance I watched my grandmother capture the hen.

'Shhhhh….'

And then she undertook that task with an air of deliberation, eyeing the victim she had chosen within the byre. Fixing on a brown-feathered bird, she took slow, careful steps towards it, her feet swishing through a thick covering of hay. At some point, her target must have guessed the direction of my grandmother's eyes. It squawked, began to flap its wings and run, but not before the woman's great hands swept down, capturing the bird in her grip. After a few kicks and spasms, it stayed still, as if the act of capture had already halted its existence. The hen seemed stiff, brown, more like a hat that might be perched on a woman's head for kirk than a living creature. It was as if it had already anticipated what might happen next – Grandma taking it to the edge of a field tall and green with oats in order to complete the deed, holding the hen's legs firmly, placing its chest on her thigh, pulling the bird's neck forward with her finger and thumb, waiting for the flapping and kicking to come to an end, her fingers relaxing when this occurred, her own hand looking as marked and wrinkled as the chicken's foot.

My sister Rachel shook her head when she saw all this, colour ebbing from her face, eyes clouding and filling.

'No,' she said.

But apart from this, there wasn't a word from her, not even the following day as we watched our grandma continue to take responsibility for it all. She performed her usual miracles above liquid, dipping the bird into hot water, making sure its feathers were doused.

'Time for a bath,' she said.

And then there was a whirl of brown feathers and white down as she plucked the bird, her fingers making circles in that storm of movements and gestures, the bird's skin pale underneath...

Rachel vanished after that – for an hour or two.

Whether it was the killing of the bird or the way our grandmother burned off the stubble of feathers by the flame burning from a capful of methylated spirits, it was hard to say. Her absence crept up on us. She was so quiet that it took an hour or so before we noticed she was gone. After a quick search of the house, Great-Uncle Calum and I went round the neighbours, asking them if she was anywhere to be seen. After a moment or two, when the curtains stopped moving, they came to the door, shaking their heads.

'No... No... We haven't seen her round these parts.'

'No. No sign.'

It was Lachie Mor, who was visiting one of our neighbours, that spotted her. Whether his eyesight was sharper than the rest after spending those years on the prairies it was difficult to tell, but he pointed to a field not far from the river where we could see a blurred outline on the ground.

'I think that's her, cuddling Niall's calf.'

We walked towards the shape, discovered he was right.

When we found her, I stretched out my hand to raise her to her feet; the two of us walking beside my great-uncle to our home.

Tormod's Journals

1914

Niall, the man who owned the calf, had been away on the mainland when the war began, and my grandfather recorded his story in the journals. Niall also spoke about it one night when he came to visit us, his grey head bowed, rubbing occasionally his light beard which my grandfather had helped to trim only a short time before. He talked of his surprise about the declaration of war, its whole dramatic nature making him wonder for a moment if life was always like that away from his croft and the island, with strange expressions like 'Tsar' and 'Kaiser' jostling into everyday conversations, words like 'Germany' and 'Austro-Hungary' familiar to people's lips.

'I was in Dingwall when the whole thing started,' Niall said as they sat beside the fire. 'Doing some county business for the first time in my life. The next thing I heard was this bugle call, some drum major sounding the "Assembly" and then the "Fall In". He did that in a few places – the Mercat Cross, in front of the National Hotel, the west end. You know the place? It soon brought the people out of doors, young men leaving shops and offices to answer the call. I don't think I've ever seen so many people in my life. There was even one fellow doing his rounds with a horse and milk cart. He just turned to me and said, "Look after that for a wee while," as he handed over the reins. And then he scurried away to report for duty, running as fast as his wee legs could carry him.'

'That must have been some moment,' Grandad said.

'Aye… It was. An utter shock to me. I didn't know what to do. I mean, would I sign up there and then for the Seaforths? Or go back home and join the Royal Naval Reserve? I knew what I wanted to do. But instead, I was standing there with this bleedin' horse. I let it go eventually and it just stood there, staring ahead, waiting for that young fellow to come back and look after it. It looked about as puzzled as I was.'

Grandad laughed. He had felt a different kind of confusion when war had been declared – their first awareness of its coming was a shout booming across croftland as, together with his father, he had worked his scythe, swaying it back and forth across a tangle of grass, making sure the rhythm was nice and even, precise and slow. In his excitement, he let it slip from his fingers, leaving it on the ground. He turned towards the house.

'Where you going?' the old man shouted.

'I'm going to find out what's happening.'

'We'll find that out soon enough. Until then, *an uair as lugha 'n naidheachd, 's ann as mò an t-sìth.* Least news, most peace.' He continued to keep his head bowed, ignoring the cries that were going on all around him. For all that the noise was increasing, his blade continued to swish through the grass, as slowly and carefully as before, reducing all that growth to a stubble in a way that the war itself had later done.

My grandfather didn't answer. He could see that, all over the village, old men and their sons were stopping their labours, gathering with one another to discuss the news that had come. He knew, too, that whatever he did at that moment, he would have made the wrong decision in his father's eyes. Such was his unpredictability. If he continued to work, he could equally well have been condemned for not finding out what was going on. As it was, his curiosity about what was afoot had been taken as an act of rebellion, a flaunting of his father's authority. Even though now that the younger man had been both a widower and a groom and felt sure he should by rights have outgrown that obedience, he knew he hadn't done so quite yet.

'Let's keep working,' his father declared.

'All right.'

It did not take long for the news to come to them. Catriona, his new wife from North Tolsta, ran across the fields towards them, her cheeks flushed and hot.

'The minister wants us to go to kirk just now. He's got some important news to give us.'

After that, there was no argument. If the minister had given instructions, there was no choice but people had to attend to his word. From all ends of the district, the men and women crowded in the direction of their kirk, those neighbours of theirs, like Iain Help and Dòmhnall Stufan, walking alongside them on the way. Some crammed around the doorway – the young men from the northern end, Am Patch and John Finlay Macleod the boat-builder from Port of Ness, who had arrived a little too late to attend the sermon and hear Macdougall, the minister, preach about the coming conflict and how the people of the island should enrol for service.

'Some things are too important to leave to others. Some things can only be done for ourselves.'

And then the words that had persuaded so many to sign up for the conflict.

'In its wisdom, the Government has recognised how urgent the need is for men. It has promised to give each man land if they sign up to serve the King in this war. Acres for them to plough and harvest. Farms will be broken up to provide this. Land for sheep and cattle to graze. Soil in which crops can be planted.'

My grandfather made drawings of what happened both then and in the following days – the young men looking smart and spruce in their new clothing, heading to sign up for the war that had just started. He sketched them standing on the quay where he travelled to collect us over twenty years later. They wore dark navy uniforms, the khaki of soldiers, as they stood and shivered on the pier. There are five brothers who accompanied Iain Help to the conflict – Alexander, Norman, Donald, William, Angus – each one tall and strong, surviving their time in Europe. There are another three Morrison brothers – Finlay, Alexander, Angus – who never came home after the war. There is even my Great-Uncle Calum. His body has a thin grey line drawn through it, clearly added in to show the illness that would afflict one side of his body just a few short weeks later.

And then there is the self-portrait of the man who was smiling as he waited there in the kirk, hoping, perhaps, that the coming days would fill the emptiness within him at that time. It had not been so very long long since his first wife, Morag, had died, since he bowed his head and accepted the choice of a new bride, Catriona, for himself. It was as if he wanted a break from that existence, as if he believed that the war would not bring loss and pain but healing, restoring a sense of calm that was gone. When he stood up from the pews that day, his stride was sure and certain. He had a confidence and a purpose he had been without since his wife had passed away.

1936

'For all that sorrow and loss has brought these children here,' Maclaren the new minister informed the family the day he arrived in our home for the first time, 'there are good things about their arrival too. Since the coming of the Great War, the people here have seen too much of the dead and dying, those who are wounded and maimed. We need young people to restore a little spirit to the place. Their energy and laughter are needed here.'

Great-Uncle Calum snorted loudly about that after the man had left. 'Oh, that explains Seònaid then,' he grinned, talking about the young woman from the district the minister had married a short time after his first wife died. Since then, he had fathered a daughter for himself, years after his two sons had left home. 'He was thinking about bringing a little energy and laughter to the place.'

Grandma ignored him, as she always did when he was in a mood to challenge her church and faith. 'He was right in what he said about these children. They have no knowledge of the Bible. That's hardly surprising when you consider.'

She and the minister had decided that after they had questioned me about some of the figures in that book.

'David?'

'Samson?'

'Goliath?'

They drew the line at mentioning Jesus or any of the disciples in case they might discover that I was past the point of salvation, unable even to recognise the one who was the Son of God.

'It's all very sad. No doubt the boy will know the names of footballers though. That's the kind of house these children were brought up in. No space for the Bible. Plenty of room for sin to creep in.'

The minister smiled, stretching out his hands in my direction. I noted that this was the first set of fingers I had seen since my arrival here that did not have a dark ring of earth under the nails. Neither were they bitten or broken like those of so many of the people here, but trimmed neatly instead. This was unlike his grey wavy hair, allowed to grow instead of being clipped short like most other men.

'Herd. McCulloch. Harkness. Massie... What team were these fellows famous playing for?'

For an instant, Grandma looked baffled, as if the minister himself was guilty of smuggling his own quantity of sin into the house.

'Hearts,' I answered.

Maclaren laughed. 'I thought you'd know that.' Turning to Grandma, he offered his own explanation of his knowledge. 'It's my son, Ronald. He's in Edinburgh. He keeps me informed of things like that.'

'Oh?' Grandma frowned.

'Not that I really approve of it. But he still goes to kirk on the Sabbath. Tynecastle the day before.'

'Aye.'

'And that's not like the home you came from, is it, Alasdair? Did your father go to kirk on the Sabbath?'

I shrugged, unwilling to give a response.

'And on a Saturday. What places did he go to then?'

Again, I refused to speak.

'Oh come on, Alasdair. Don't be insolent to the minister. You know it's not like you.'

Nothing.

'Alasdair?'

'Third Lanark. Clyde. Rangers. Celtic. Anyone that Aberdeen was playing against in Glasgow.'

I remembered again my father's ebullience on such occasions, especially when Aberdeen won. That team's gold and black scarf draped around his neck, he would serenade us with the words of his favourite song, 'Loch Lomond', again and again, telling me that 'the hale stadium was singing' when Matt Armstrong or his hero, Willie Mills, scored. 'It was great, great, great.' He'd whirl Rachel round and round, listening to her cries of 'Again, Daddy, again,' as he waltzed her through our home. I loved him fiercely as I watched him do this, thinking he was the most wonderful father in existence.

My words did not have the same effect on the minister. He frowned, his forehead gathering as many strands as my grandad's hay-fork when he was setting out fodder for his horses.

'Oh, I see. The pity I have for any man who encourages his children to worship eleven ordinary men instead of the Father, Son and Holy Ghost. Tell me: did your school make up for these deficiencies in any way?'

'Deficencies?' I faltered at the word.

'Oh.' He laughed at his own error. 'Did they teach you the Psalms?'

I shook my head.

'Catechism?'

Again, I shook my head in response.

'What about Bible stories?'

I had a vague recollection of my father lifting a tin of Lyle's Golden Syrup one morning and speaking about the picture of a dead lion that was drawn upon it, and something about the strong coming from the sweet, but I couldn't be sure where the tale came from. So I stayed dumb, listening instead to my grandad speak for the first time at the table. He cleared his throat, coughing before he heaved out the words.

'To be fair, the lad's a little young for things like the catechism.'

The minister shook his head sadly. 'Oh, Tormod, you're never too young for things like that. Prayer and psalm should be part of your being from the moment you're in the cradle. After all, as someone who was on that dark ship that New Year's morning, you should know better than most you never know the day or the hour. And you must always be prepared for it. Always certain of your soul's destination the instant that death comes. And that applies not only for you, but even more surely for the children who are among us.'

Grandad flinched as these words were spoken, his face chilling and body shaking the way it had when he had come across the explosion at the edge of the moor.

'But rest assured,' the minister continued, 'they will soon be prepared for the time that death might arrive for them.

Miss McKerracher is well versed in the Scripture. She knows too how a child's heart needs to be fortified with prayer. It will not be long before verses of psalm and paraphrase will be tripping from their tongues.' He tapped my grandad's fingers with an outstretched hand. 'And that will be good for the entire household. We all need to be ringed with the resilience of faith.'

It wasn't too long till I arrived there – my new school with all its strangeness after the old one where I had been previously. Much smaller than that building, the headmaster's house was attached to the other end of it; his wife growing potatoes and vegetables – carrots, cabbages and leeks – alongside our playground, ivy growing up the outside wall. The presence of these fruits and crops seemed almost as exotic as her English accent when she called out for her husband sometimes to bring him to their kitchen for a scone and a cup of tea.

'Roderick! It's ready…'

The boys squirmed and giggled when they heard her yell, imitating her voice.

'My mum said she's from London…'

'Rochdale,' another argued.

'Same thing really.'

'Apparently they met at the theatre together. She said that anyway to my mum. Whatever a theatre is.'

And then they raced away, a bunch of lads dressed in thick sweaters and shorts, jostling against one another as they ran, Gaelic shouts coming from their lips. It was their legs and feet I noticed most. Some of them didn't have any shoes; others had tiny little cuts and burns below their knees. This didn't seem to matter when they played football on the stony slope behind the school. They bustled and shoved, giving each other no quarter in their hurry to kick the ball.

Yet, of all things, it was the memorised questions and answers of the catechism that I found strangest and most disconcerting about my new school. Miss McKerracher stood in front of the class when we recited them in the morning. A globe on her desk, a map of the world with wide stretches of red, she was dressed in her tweed suit and grey cardigan. Her black cloak flapped as she hurled her questions in the direction of my fellow seven- and eight-year-olds. With her dark hair and intense brown eyes, she looked as much like a raven as she did a human being, that span of black a stretch of wings. She only flapped a little when she came to me, finding my surname difficult to pronounce when she read out the register, an alien sound among the Macleods, Morrisons and Murrays.

'Cr-oooooo-kshank,' she said, stretching out my second name into three or four syllables, a sound I heard all my classmates imitating over the next few weeks. ('Croo-iii-ookshank. Crooooooookshank. Crooooo-iiiii-kkkshank.') She smiled. 'I think I'll be calling you Alasdair, though there's quite a few of them.'

Otherwise she was both tentative and gentle with me, asking an easy question during those first days I sat in that class, for all that my response made very little sense to my mind.

'*What is the chief end of man?*'

Eventually I learned the reply. '*Man's chief end is to glorify God, and to enjoy him forever.*'

'Very good.' It was then she truly began, whirling round

to face some of the older pupils in the room. '*What special act of providence did God exercise toward man in the estate wherein he was created?*' she asked.

And then the response came back from the class, chanted in a single voice.

'*When God had created man, he entered into a covenant of life with him, upon condition of perfect obedience; forbidding him to eat of the tree of the knowledge of good and evil, upon the pain of death.*'

After that, she whirled round again, focusing on a single person, her finger prodding out the words like a beak tapping.

'Murdo? *Did our first parents continue in the estate wherein they were created?*'

I looked across at Murdo. Sitting alongside me, a short, tubby, fair-haired boy muttered his response. It was slow and faltering, as if the words were strangling in his throat.

'*Our first parents...*'

'*Being left to the freedom...*' the teacher prompted.

'*Being left to the freedom...*' Murdo repeated. '*Of their own will...*'

'*Fell from the estate...*' Miss McKerracher said.

'*Fell from the estate ... wherein they were created...*'

'*By sinning against God,*' the teacher announced triumphantly. 'You didn't learn it, did you?'

'No.'

'That's sad,' she declared. 'After all the chances you've had. Come out here.'

Miss McKerracher walked to her desk, higher than the ones in which the rest of us sat, and opened the lid. A moment later and, turning to face the boy in front of her, she took out a thin coil of leather.

'Stretch out your hands.'

I winced as the belt came down on his hands – again and again and again.

It was then I thought of my own parents. My mother's cough. My father's whisky-clouded breath, the way he used to reel when he had taken a drink or two too many in the Hayburn or the Dolphin. It seemed to me that Miss McKerracher has been talking about them. Words tumbled from my lips as I heard the whack of the belt against the boy's skin.

'No!' I shouted. 'They didn't fall! They didn't fall.'

'Sorry?'

'They didn't fall,' I continued to insist.

'Alasdair… Master Cruickshank…'

And that's when she lost control of the class, stammering out an explanation of what she meant by mankind falling, listening – for the first time – to the muttering of children around the room.

Tormod's Journals

The Great War

It wasn't the war my grandfather wrote mainly about in his journals, that aversion of his to blood and killing we saw that day when the hen was slaughtered clear in his work.

Instead, he wrote about his sister, Christina, how she had to be taken away after she attacked his father, scraping the side of his neck with a knife. His other sister, Eilidh, sent letters to him often, telling him of other incidents, writing out her thoughts in her neat precise script. He could imagine Eilidh's still, placid face giving no indication of her feelings as she wrote, all hidden away like her black hair under the tight knot of her scarf. It was as if she existed behind a succession of walls, each one more impenetrable than the last, preventing the intrusion of the remainder of the world.

Christina is the same as ever. The other day she got into a big fight with Father about wanting to plough up the field to plant the potatoes. He refused, of course, told her it was no work for a woman, but she kept on arguing, showing her arms and shouting, 'Do you not think I'm strong enough? Do you not think I'm almost as strong as you?'

Tormod could easily picture Christina like that, rolling up

her sleeves and showing the sinews that mapped her arms, a tight network of veins and arteries all clear and vivid below the whiteness of her skin. Or she might display her hands; all knots and knuckles, blisters, bruises and cuts, each wound she had gained during her work on either croft or harbour on display. There was even a gash where the blade of her penknife had slipped once while she was gutting fish on the harbour, tearing into the base of her thumb.

She was right in one of her arguments. She was almost as strong as her father, if not more so. Her shoulders dipped and rose as she worked for hours in the fields. Her feet, too, moved quickly as though she were dancing an arc across stubble. Yet despite this grace, there was much about her that seemed manly to Tormod. Her fair hair was often bedraggled and untidy, a sheen of sweat constantly glowing on her face and arms. Unlike most of the other women around her, she seemed to have little sense of cleanliness or hygiene. A sour smell – one that belonged more to the sea than soil – accompanied her wherever she walked. It mingled blood and seaweed, mud and manure. There were times when he was away when he was reminded of her – in a beggar sitting in a doorway in Rouen, her hair straggled and dirty; the time he had sailed to Sierra Leone and seen the dark and hungry people there; a young woman from a munitions factory he met while taking a cargo of artillery shells back to the ship. Her face had a haunted, jaundiced quality; her fingers were yellow with the powder they used to prepare the explosives. It was as if the nature of her work had poisoned and infected her, seeping out of her skin. In Christina's case, there was something similar. Her madness bled from her, tainting all those who came into contact with her. There was little shock or surprise when he received a letter from his wife one day.

She had to go, for all that we are all very sad about it.
They took her over to Stornoway where they put her on
the boat, the Sheila, for the mainland. She'll be there for
a very long time. If she ever gets out of hospital at all.

He drew Christina on Stornoway pier – the place he only saw for the second time in his life when he signed up for the war. Her hands are tied and knotted together with rope. Her head, beneath her shawl, dips low. He wondered if she had any notion of where she was going or where she had been. They probably took her on a boat from the small village of Skigersta to the town, her father by her side, a curse upon her lips every time she turned in his direction. 'Take your hands off me. What makes you think I want a finger of yours lying upon me?' And then there was her destination – the hospital outside Inverness with its high walls and a green borderline of trees. Tormod had seen it for the first time when the train passed through that Highland town on its way to the naval base in Invergordon at the beginning of the war. He'd shut his eyes, a shudder passing through him like so many others who had signed up for the conflict, all with relatives either inside the building or whose behaviour made it likely that they might one day end up there.

And then there was the time that Calum came home, stepping down the gangway to the exact same pier, rejecting all offers of help; even his father's hand when it was stretched out towards him, nearly striking him – like all the others

– with his walking stick, shouting the words that had gone down in the family folklore.

'You think I'm a bloody invalid? What makes you think I need your bloody arm to cling on to?'

Yet there are glimpses in the pages of the journals of how my grandfather felt about the conflict, especially being a seaman on the *Aboukir,* the ancient cruiser on which he first served. It was an old, decrepit vessel unfit for the wiles and tricks of either wave or war, and he sketched and wrote about the dirt and the crammed nature of the vessel: eating in the same mess where they slept with barely an inch of space between hammocks; breathing in the stink of oil, grease and cordite; the occasional hiss of steam from a broken, rusted pipe; hearing too the remorseless chug of the engine when it worked or, all too often, its quiet or muffled noise – as something went wrong below deck. Occasionally, too, he drew the ocean, the manner in which it shook every sense in his body – pitching, swaying, surging, heaving, rolling, making his eyes pulse, forcing him to be sick over the leeward rail, the salt swallowed by his mouth as he bent over.

And then there would be the moments of calm, the times when both sky and sea took on a strange and circular stillness, when it was hard to believe you were moving. The crewmen sometimes stood there and listened to that ominous silence, fearing that at a moment like this one of the enemy destroyers might appear, punishing their stillness with a salvo of guns, the firing of torpedoes.

'We're bloody live bait,' Massie, in the next hammock, said one night. 'That's all we flipping are.'

'I don't think anyone would be interested in blinking swallowing us,' someone nearby retorted. 'Too damn old and tasteless.'

'Don't you believe it. They'll chew us up and spit us out.'

Even the dampness and sweat of other men's bodies, the foulness of their presence engrained in both their clothes and blankets, provided proof of the ship's deep and inner decay. They grumbled continually in discontent – about the quality of their food, the nature of their officers, including the captain, Drummond. There were times when Tormod would try and escape this, standing on the deck and gulping the strong winds blowing across the ocean. It allowed him an occasional glimpse of a world where there was a wider horizon, where life was less narrow and confined. If he had pencil and paper at that time, there would have been much for him to sketch – the wings of gulls as they followed the ship, the black and white back of a whale breaking the surface, the fin of a dolphin. Sights he had rarely seen during his years working in the smithy, hammering away at the rim of a wheel, fixing a horse-shoe on the hoof of the mare, a cloud of steam obscuring his vision of the landscape that stretched around him, the farmhouse and the manse, the river that powered the mill-wheel from time to time.

Yet even as he stood there on deck, he was always conscious that there might be the glint and presence of steel, a German vessel making its way in their direction. That feeling haunted him when he was stood on the foredeck one stormy morning when they were sailing out of Harwich, near the Broad Fourteens, a patch of the Dutch coast in the southern part of the North Sea. The *Aboukir* was travelling more slowly than usual, wheezing a path through the seas, the black of the sky fading to the grey of a September dawn. The vessel not zigzagging as it was supposed to do, saving coal its ancient engines gobbled down. One of the officers told them not to worry about this. The seas would be causing problems for the enemy too. They, too, would be crippled and thwarted by the waves. Besides, the *Aboukir* and the *Hogue* and *Cressy* nearby all had look-outs peering out into the mist for periscopes, guns manned on either side of the ship. No worries. No dangers. No trouble in sight.

And then the torpedo struck, a trail of bubbles breaking the surface of the water, popping and bursting as it sped along, giving a sense of the ship scraping over a large stick. There was a whistle, too, through the water, a sound Tormod thought at first he was imagining and tried to shake from his head.

'*Dè? Dè tha tachairt?*'

The Gaelic words had come quickly and naturally to his lips as he turned to face one of the other sailors, a tiny Englishman they all called Charlie Ellis. The other Naval Reserveman's response – 'Think we've hit a bloody mine' – was silenced by the boom of an explosion. It struck the vessel amidships below the waterline.

'Damn! Damn! Damn!'

The sirens went off, howling in the darkness. Lights swirling on the deck. The boiler room and engines had been hit, grinding the vessel to a halt. From below, there rose a pillar of thick smoke, tongues of flame, a torrent of water, scald of steam. Tormod felt the deck shift below his feet as the vessel listed to port. Looking up, he saw that Drummond had decided they had been hit by a mine and was hoisting the warning signal aloft. Tormod shook his head in disbelief, aware that the captain was wrong. That line of bubbles had not been the work of any mine. Instead, the danger had come from below, the dark hulk of a submarine lying like a steel rock in the depths, concealed below the stormy surface of the waves. He was reminded of its impact years later, when another vessel – taking him homewards – struck the rocks just outside Stornoway. At this moment, he felt just as dumbfounded as he would on the *Iolaire*, unable to yell in protest at the stupidity of those who were in command over him. Drummond was asking the other two ships – the *Hogue* and *Cressy* nearby – to come to their rescue.

'What the hell are you doing, man?' he heard Ellis yell by his side. 'Don't you know there are U-boats about?'

'Jesus Christ!'

The world shifted again. Drummond had given orders for apartments on the port side of the *Aboukir* to be flooded, to right and steady the boat. All it did was make the cruiser pitch once more, the waves swelling closer to the deck, more fierce and white than the worst winter Tormod had ever experienced home on the island. He knew that they would devour men, as surely as cold or hunger did, swallowing up their lives. He looked up to see that only one lifeboat was available. Others had been smashed or the winching gear had been broken, no steam-power there to haul and hoist them down to the waves. He glanced around to see if there were any spars – broken, perhaps, in the blast – to which he could cling when the ship finally went down. One or two were in his eyeline. Places to which he could run when the inevitable call to abandon ship was made.

It didn't take long to happen. A half-hour or so later and Tormod was in the ocean, two stretches of wood underneath his arms keeping him afloat in the water. All around him, there was the black sheen and stink of oil. He smothered himself in it, a mighty swipe that tasted foul and blinded him for a while, but he knew that it would keep him warm in the chill of these waters. He was almost concealed in it, a stain among the waves, as he watched the *Aboukir* go down, its freshly painted bottom red and bright on the surface for a while. The sight tempted men to swim towards it in the hope that its bulk and weight would stay afloat, allowing them to stay alive until a ship would pick them up in a few hours' time. They managed this for a short while, dark figures on scarlet, trembling as they clung or balanced on steel, determined that they would be saved, but then the *Aboukir* turned once again. These old hands slipped from perches as it swirled deeper under water, a dark plume of smoke as it sank into the depths, its heat sparking off a cloud of steam.

And that wasn't all Tormod saw from his place within the waves. He saw the *Hogue* slow down as its captain realised there was a submarine in these waters, aware that Drummond had got it wrong when he flagged up there were mines within this stretch of sea. He saw, too, how the crew of the *Cressy* failed to recognise the danger, making its way quickly towards the *Aboukir*. It was an error they recognised only when the first torpedo hit them – that tell-tale line of bubbles scarring the waves once again, small, insignificant eruptions that preceded the fire to come, the blaze and column of smoke that spiralled from its starboard side, curling round the boat. A moment or two later, it was followed by another one, which narrowly missed her stern. After that, a further torpedo was fired in the *Cressy's* direction. It blasted its side, causing the vessel to sink. Even though his sight was smeared and darkened by oil, Tormod closed his eyes. He could see that no lifeboat had slipped away from her, that just about everyone on board was dead, all those he knew, officers, able seamen and lascars alike, disappearing in the fire and heat. He heard himself repeating one line from the Psalms in the Bible his new wife insisted that they read together every night.

'*Yea, though I walk through the valley of the shadow of death, yet shall I fear no evil.*'

He was picked up a few hours later, trembling and shaking, by a trawler that had sailed out to their rescue. He remembered sitting there with some of the other men the fishermen had lifted from the waters. They looked – he thought – like starlings that gathered some mornings on the thatch of his home in South Dell, black, shining and naked, huddled together to keep themselves warm. Even their voices sounded like the noises these birds sometimes made. Arching their necks, heads bobbing up and down, they muttered and mumbled, let out an occasional groan, their mouths and teeth chirping in the cold, a chorus of complaint and despair. It was as if they had stopped being individuals but had, in the face of the enormity of the suffering they had experienced, become something tribal, a crew that had come together in the horror of the previous hours, not allowing any space or distance to come between them, motivated by the fear that if they let any more of their number perish, they might all slip away.

That feeling stayed with him over much of the next few days. He remembered how his fingers trembled when he thought back over all that had happened. How he cried – like so many of the others – for hours on end. How, when he spoke, his voice was parched and slurred with tiredness. Carried somehow within the pores of his skin, perhaps even in the core of his soul, there was the depth of darkness below the keel of the *Aboukir*. The stench of oil that came from all of them – their uniforms torn and black with grease, segments of cloth torn from their legs and backs. The savage bite of sickness in his throat.

And even when all that passed – when his sense of himself was restored by the touch of a nurse, the clasp of a doctor's hand on his back – he never quite forgot the sense of his own fragility which had come to him that September morning, the thought that all his life was frail and breakable, easily smashed and destroyed by a torpedo surging through the waters towards them, an unexpected rock below the surface, the blast of a shell, even the hail of bullets riddling flesh and steel.

1936

'It was his sister we were worried about. All her wandering. Her refusal to speak. We thought, of the two of them, he was the one coping better,' Grandad said the day he came to school. 'He's always smiling, watching, interested in what's going on. Not like his sister, who doesn't say anything. Rarely a word since she arrived. I thought she was the one who missed her father the most. Drawn to the shadows by her mother's loss.'

Or at least that's how I imagined the conversation taking place. It was one that became familiar to me as an adult, during my years of teaching. There would be some incident inside a classroom. Some boy toppling over his desk, swearing and cursing at either one of his fellow pupils or a member of staff. The kicking of a paint can. The wielding of an artist's knife. And then there would be the parents coming into the classroom, proffering an explanation of what had gone wrong in the child's life. How the father (or mother) had left the house, going off with one of the next-door neighbours. How a gran or grandad had just died or gone to hospital. How someone in the family, perhaps an older brother, had been sentenced to a spell in prison for an act of theft or vandalism. There might even be the suggestion that you as a teacher should have been more sensitive to the child's distress, anticipating his or her reaction to an event that had taken place outside your immediate awareness or knowledge, that you hadn't been focused enough on their offspring's needs, distracted by the presence of another twenty-odd individuals – some also angry and troubled – in the room.

But these kind of conversations would occur in different times. Instead, my grandad would nod his head at whatever Miss McKerracher did or said, not mentioning how I had never come across the Shorter Catechism with all its odd questions and commands, how I had never seen the belt being wielded in my Glasgow primary school, how I had been terrified by the strangeness of the world into which I'd stepped.

'He isn't used to it,' Grandad would probably have said, as if a child ought to become accustomed to the sight of a teacher whacking a strip of leather across a younger, smaller person's fingers. 'That's why he shouted at Miss McKerracher that day, that's why he reacted like that.'

But behind that classroom talk, I would be aware there was a different kind of conversation, one that would go on behind the hands of the teachers. The headmaster might point out that strange behaviour was almost the normal custom in our family. They would recall my grandad's sister, Christina, and the way they had been forced to take her away soon after the war started.

'There's a crack in some of them,' the headteacher, Roderick MacAskill, might mutter, his manner as loud and theatrical as ever. 'One that's been there for years. You remember how Christina used to act, how she threw a knife at her father?'

They might nod then, mentioning too the fervency of my grandma's prayers and how her voice could be heard from the end of the barn, urging God to look after her natural son away in the village of North Tolsta on the other side of the moor; asking Him, too, to heal us after all the hurt and breakage that the last few years had caused in our lives. To be fair, we were not the only ones in that situation. Many others were mentioned in the long litany of names I heard echoing in the darkness.

Through my grandma's words, I became conscious of all the loss and absence within the village and indeed the island as a whole, the reason for the twitching of net curtains, the hope, perhaps, that ghosts would be glimpsed once again. Their number included the dead from the war, from that time when the world had been tipped out of balance and never quite set upright again. Sometimes it was those who were abroad who were spoken about. Grandma's own brother, Murdo Dan. Her sister, Mary, and her husband, Lachlan. Sometimes it was those who were unknown to me that were mentioned in her mutterings, part of a legion who had travelled to either the States or Canada many years before. They told of their whereabouts through either photographs or postcards. The Golden Gate of San Francisco. New York harbour. Halifax, Nova Scotia. There was one neighbour called Jessie who used to press a postcard of a tree on me every time I went past her house. A large, broad woman whose white hair contrasted with her black widow's clothes, she would snatch the postcard out from its place on the dresser, ready for her to show to anyone who came to the door.

'Look at it, *ille*,' she would say. 'That's what a tree looks like... The cedars of Lebanon. The palm tree that Zachariah climbed to see our Lord. The one that Judas Iscariot hanged himself from. That's what one of them looks like.'

Some of the villagers – the ones who had been in Stornoway and seen the woodland in the castle grounds – used to smile at that, the sharp, rapid way in which she stammered out this information, but they were still impressed by the size and stature of that sepia-shaded tree. Its trunk seemed massive. Its branches stretched wide as the cliff-face on the village shoreline. Perched among them, there was a man with a black moustache; his face and much of his chest obscured by leaves as he sat upright among its expanse. His mother would prod a finger in his direction, especially when in the company of those whose sight was a little dull and blurred.

'There's a man in there... Can you see him?'

It was her son Roddy who had posted it from the States a number of years before. It was his message, too, that was scrawled on its back.

My dearest family,

I am writing to tell you that I am getting along fine here in America. Things are going well for me in the new grocer's shop I am working in. I am learning the names of all the strange fruit and vegetables that are on sale here. It's odd to think that I'm selling things like peaches, pears and bananas, which I had never even seen before I left home. The thing I miss most of all is the sound of our own Gaelic. No one has spoken to me in that tongue for months – though there is an Irishman

who works with me who speaks something similar to it.
Hope you like the picture. I will send you more of things
you haven't had the chance to see where you live.

With all my affection,

   Your loving son,

     Roddy

My great-uncle used to laugh and say it was her son that
was hiding there, playing hide and seek among the foliage.
He would pretend he could spot things that seemed familiar
– Roddy's collarless shirt, dark trousers, the pair of boots he
had bought with the first wage obtained as a storekeeper.
Calum would let on that he could see Roddy's barrel-like
chest, too large for his small and slender frame, that black
moustache he had grown since crossing the Atlantic. 'A fine,
black, bushy one,' he told his mother. 'Grand enough for any
soldier.' There was the same shyness, too, the boy had always
possessed. Glancing down, he was staring at the black boots
clinging precariously to the branch he was standing upon, as
if he didn't quite belong in that perch high above the earth,
and was anxious that the moment was coming when he
would come crashing down to land.

Yet Calum never told her what he muttered in my
direction once – that, with every passing year, her son
was becoming fainter. It was difficult to tell how this was
happening. Perhaps the leaves were becoming thicker and
fuller. Or the clouds in the background were merging with
its branches, becoming less distinct from one another as,

with each passing year, the tree grew higher in the sky. Or it might have been the few rays of sun that passed through the doorway of the blackhouse draining shape and form from that photograph, until it became impossible to tell whether it was man or woman that was balancing there. Or an angel's glow as the man moved further from the realm of their existence, just like her son and Roddy's older brother, Finlay, who, Great-Uncle Calum told me, had been killed when the *Iolaire* went down in Stornoway harbour. Roddy was a different sort of ghost now, one trapped in another continent, far away from the borders of their world.

Yet mostly it was those who had lost their lives in the conflict or even afterwards that people mentioned. Or that ship they only mentioned in whispers, the *Iolaire*, as if the very mention of its name was a curse that fell upon their lips from time to time. And then there would be the way Great-Uncle Calum would nod to all the black-clothed widows and spinsters he met as he limped along the road, whispering to me some detail of their lives.

'That's Mairead. Her husband, Jock, was killed in the Med.'

'Murdag… Her husband, he was on the *Iolaire*.'

'Dolina lost three of her brothers in the war. Never been right since.'

Sometimes those we passed looked tearful, as if they had passed the hours of darkness thinking of their loss, unconsoled by the words they had read in the Bible meant to provide them with comfort, weeping through the night.

There was one man I remembered both Calum and my grandad speaking about. I heard him one morning, just after our cockerel had stopped crowing and became settled for the day. He was shouting and cursing a short distance away, making his way to the post office with his walking stick clutched in his hand.

'Who's that?' I asked.

'It's Angus. He's not been right since the war.'

I pressed them both a little on this, gaining splinters of information from them both. My grandad saying that two of his brothers had been killed at the Battle of Coronel. Angus had been on the *Glasgow* off the Chilean coast when the *Monmouth* and *Good Hope* had gone down, aware that his brothers were on the second of these boats, fire and sea engulfing them despite all the height and power of the Andes sheltering the harbour only a short distance away. He had seen the funnels of his brothers' vessel lit up by white flame burning below the bridge, the green stars of the explosives on board shooting upwards to the evening sky as it sank downwards, the forward section of the vessel breaking off from the rest and tumbling into the sea. Moments later there was only the low shadow of its hull, illuminated by the red glare of oil burning on the waves around the wreckage.

'Imagine, watching your two brothers being killed and not being able to do a thing about it,' Calum said.

Angus' shouting continued like an echo of that evening. He was yelling and calling, cursing the others on his ship for leaving his two brothers in the water and never going to their aid.

'You bastards! You bastards! Why don't you try and save my brothers, you bastards?'

Sometimes the war would reverberate in different ways. Occasionally, on our way to or from school, we would meet someone who had been wounded in the conflict. There was a man whose leg had been lopped off in some battle on land or sea; we never asked which. Another's nose had gone astray, ripped off by a bullet or explosion. One, too, whose mouth was twisted, making it hard for him to either talk or eat. A thin, gangling man called Ruairidh, with a nose that resembled the beaks of the swans that sometimes thronged the lochs of the district. He wore dressings – tight around his chest – that had clearly not been changed for a while, dried blood staining the edge of cloth peeking from his shirt. He would come sometimes to our house to talk to my grandad and Calum, his face and fingers often shining with a layer of grease from the mutton he would often eat, both in our house and elsewhere. My nose would wrinkle when he was with us, especially when he sat a short distance from the fire, the mix of his sweat and sheep-fat adding to the potency of the smell. Rachel's face grew chilled and pale, as if she was always on the verge of being sick when he was nearby. My grandad's forehead knotted, the dark star on his cheek crinkling, when he saw our reaction.

'He was the first sent home from the front in these parts. People gripped his hand and grinned when they saw him, calling him a hero. It didn't take long for that to change. Especially when others began to join him. Soon they disliked him being around, complaining about the smell he carried round with him everywhere. It's as if he thrust in our faces exactly what was going on in France and elsewhere. And people didn't want to be reminded of that.'

Instead of lessening, that reaction probably became worse as the decades went on. There was a sense of another conflict coming. I heard my Great-Uncle Calum talking about it with his friends as they met in each other's homes. Mostly they spoke about the movement of sheep across the moor, how some crofter or another had a flock that invariably wandered to some section or other of its emptiness, how too some animal had drowned in a bog – with Calum invariably being the one to be the bearer of that news. And then there was a litany of names – Hitler, Mussolini, Germany, Stalin, Japan – that kept edging its way into conversation. They'd shake their heads each time they uttered them, as if they could sense the damage all these men and the countries would do to this earth.

'As if we haven't seen enough,' one of them said. 'As if there hasn't been enough loss in these parts.'

Tormod's Journals

December 1918

There was a confession folded away in one of my grandfather's journals, a few soaked, salt-stained sheets of paper he must have written during the nights and days before he returned from the war – scribbled notes and drawings he kept inside an oilcloth package telling of how the closer that he came to home, the more he remembered both sparks and the stink of cow-dung. The first was drawn in countless little sketches of the trade to which he would have to return when he arrived home. Dark tongs being cooled and doused in water. Sparks struck off an anvil. The continual whack and impact of a hammer on iron. Recollections inspired by Eilidh's letter when Calum became paralysed on one side.

Our father says to tell you you'll have to be the
blacksmith now. There is no choice.

And shit too. There are constant drawings of that substance, caked on the backsides of cattle, little deposits left upon the grass, smearing, too, the soles and uppers of his boots, wads of straw thick with the stuff becoming embedded in his clothing, the sleeves of his jackets; his trouser-ends attracting, too, the yellow dung flies that clustered on horse, cattle and sheep muck littering ground, bracken, heather. It is as if he wanted to familiarise himself with it, provide little reminders to himself that in a few days' time, now that the conflict was over, he would be back among it, cleaning out the byre that stood at the end of his father's home instead of swabbing and washing the decks of the *Glengarry*, swishing them clean, checking that – if the occasion demanded – the barrel of each gun was clean enough for salvo and shell to whistle through. He would wield his three-pronged dung-fork as well as he used a pencil or a long-handled scrubber on deck, shovelling shit and straw into a wheelbarrow, heaving this out, too, to the heap behind his home where he would hear the slap of dung against dung, shit against shit, as he emptied his load on top of the one he had gathered the previous day. And all the time, his back and shoulders would be aching. The acrid smell of urine would fill his nostrils, gagging in his throat.

There would be a gathering of flies like the ones he drew that morning as he sat on the pavement outside Inverness railway station, his back against his kitbag next to the outside wall of the Station Hotel. Brown and black. Midges and bigger ones, those that settled on both milk and meat. Thousands of them would be swarming round his face on still summer evenings, when he had no free hand to swat them away, his grip tight and sure on the wheelbarrow's handles. Even if he could raise his arm, there was the thought that his skin would be smeared with cow-shit if he smacked one, dirt remaining on his cheek or forehead till he had the chance to wipe it clean.

The hell with it. He tried to wash his anger from his mind, concentrating instead on sketching his last few glimpses of the world he was set to leave behind. He made small, brisk pencil strokes on the sheets of paper propped upon his lap, outlining a few of the objects and figures he could see. The clock above the station entrance. The Cameron statue in the centre of the square. The crowd of men in their uniforms, dark naval collars and bell bottoms, huddling around the doorway of the Highland Railway office as they waited to go home to take in the New Year in places like Stornoway, Tarbert, Portree. They laughed at the English, who had all chosen to go home for Christmas and were now back on board ship again. Around them all, the sound of music ebbed and swelled, echoing from the man they called the Forres Fiddler as he played for the returning servicemen inside the station or for the lips of his fellow islanders as they sang their Gaelic songs. There was even one man – a fellow called Jockie – who pranced upon the pavement, performing his own version of a tune Tormod had heard all too often during his years away.

> '*It's a long way to Portnaguran,*
> *It's a long way to go...*'

For all that he did not share his spirit, Tormod grinned at the man's antics, the way that he sang this song and another one he called 'Iain Murdo, won't you please come home?'. In truth, his own home was not somewhere to which he longed to return. Instead, he sickened each time he thought about it, recalling how it felt the last time he was home on furlough or when he had his period of rest and recovery after the *Aboukir* had gone down. His daughter shy of his approach, cleaving more to Catriona than she ever did to him. His wife foreign and strange. His father wild and furious. Looking back at his life there, it seemed to him a place without grace or sweetness. One in which Calum limped around, dragging the right side of his body, fated to be crippled all his days. One to which Catriona belonged, her thoughts and feelings as tightly coiled and controlled as the grey bun upon her head. One in which his father still swaggered round like the harshest and most unpredictable of kings, barking out contradictory instructions in the direction of his son.

'Whoa! Whoa! Don't pile the barrow up quite so high! Better one more trip out to the byre than a back that's out of kilter...'

Yet if he ever tried to put a little less on his load, the older man would shake his head.

'Steady on! Steady on! You can put some more in it than that.'

There would be nothing contradictory, however, about the way his father would react to what Tormod was doing now. He could imagine the man padding over in his direction, the puff of his breath as he sneaked a glance over his son's shoulder, noting the detail he was adding to the drawing of the Cameron statue he had etched out on the page.

'What are you wasting your time on that nonsense for?'

He blew on his fingers, clenching his fists, trying once again to concentrate on his drawing. It was harder than ever to do now that he had noticed John Macdermid skulking on the edges of the men gathered on the opposite side of the square. The Harrisman had been on the *Glengarry* with him for most of the war, his dark face menacing him with quotations from the Bible every time he picked up his pencil to try and draw, his brown eyes as sharp and judgemental as the Shorter Catechism he had learned at school. *What is forbidden in the seventh commandment? The seventh commandment forbiddeth all unchaste thoughts, words and actions.* Tormod did the same now as he had done back then, ignoring the man's mutterings and warnings. Instead, he heard only the words of approval from the others around him as his pencil glided and rubbed across the page, noting the folds of the stone kilt the figure was wearing, the fine detail of the rifle that was hanging from his hand.

'That's good. God... I wish I could do the likes of that.'

There would be nothing like that when he reached home. No artistry. No release. Just days and days of listening to the same voices, working on the same tasks. His world would be a continuous shade of brown – the shade of peat on his fingers as both he and his father worked out on the moor with all its miles of heather, the colour of rotting straw and dung, the splattering on the hind-quarters of his cattle. The only contrast in shade would be the black and red of anvil and forge, the unrelenting rhythm of the hammer in his grasp.

And that would be it. So different from the pattern of the days he had spent on the *Glengarry.* So different, too, from his first ship, the *Aboukir,* which he had been on before, the one that he tried not to think about when recalling the war. On the *Glengarry,* all seemed still and peaceful. There was one occasion when the captain had ordered the guns to fire at what he believed was a U-boat a short distance out from Rosyth, only to discover it was a whale, its carcass scarred and broken by shells, the stink of scorched blubber remaining in the air for ages. On another occasion, off the coast of Antrim, they narrowly missed a row of mines the Germans had placed in those waters. He had seen one close by as they moved away, marvelling as the vessel avoided it.

Only the places that the ship sailed towards altered during his time on board. There were the visits to different ports: Leith; the London dockyards where he had been a week or two before, loading munitions from Silvertown; the times they sailed to Rouen bringing stores to the men stationed there. Trying always to dodge and avoid the German U-boats and ships, the sea-mines that might be skulking in deep or shallow waters. And throughout these voyages, the many different sights and scenes. Light upon the water. Dusk upon the land. The grey docks encountered; the shingle on the shoreline; the wind-worn, salt-blown harbour buildings; the rocking, creaking boats tied up at the quay. The different accents and languages he had heard around these places. The hours, too, spent at sea with men like John Macdermid accompanying him on watch. At first, he had spoken to him, but over time, he had grown weary of his unrelenting confidence, the warnings he doled out daily on his tongue.

'I'll tell you, Tormod, it's shocked me. How little these others know of their Bible. They'll suffer for their ignorance one of these days. The man that wandereth out of the way of understanding shall remain in the congregation of the dead.'

It was at times like these it was good to know he could escape into sheets of paper and draw. The longer Macdermid's words and sermons stretched to match the length of his face, the more likely Tormod was to pick up a piece of paper and begin to sketch something he had seen. A rope coiled upon the deck. Young Frenchwomen gutting fish on the quayside.

A group of stevedores leaning over a fire they had built under a lean-to in the dockyard. The lascars with their dark and curious faces, their even more curious beliefs. There was even the occasion he drew the procession bearing the coffin of Lord Roberts, the former British Commander-in-Chief, being carried to a boat at the quay at Boulogne. Carried by four soldiers, still stained with mud from the trenches, the box looked tiny and insignificant, as if it were impossible that a man's corpse might be within. A band played to accompany the slow progression to the boat.

All of this had been recorded on a blank sheet of paper he had discovered somewhere on ship. His pencil reached into every part of the page, covering its corners with quick, hurried lines. John Macdermid noticed him doing this and uttered words he could all too easily imagine coming from his own father's lips.

'What are you wasting your time on that nonsense for? All you're providing for people is a mirror. A way of looking at their own appearance. There's nothing more terrible than that.'

He took out his Bible from his pocket, shaking his head as he did so.

'You'd be much better off with this. A mirror for men's souls. One that allows them to see into them rather than looking at their own outer selves,' he declared. 'I've been taking the chance to learn as much of it as I can during my time on duty. Learning it off by heart.'

That might have been the end of it if Foster hadn't appeared. The Second Mate on the *Glengarry* had noticed Tormod the day Roberts had been carried to the boat and was the one, too, responsible for the precise and accurate way Tormod drew later, conscious of the effect of light and shade, the artistry and effort that was needed to draw well. The Irishman had crept up on him while he stood on watch one evening on the deck of the small, converted coaster, drawing the lighthouse on a headland their vessel was passing in the half-light of dusk. He hadn't heard the tall, broad-shouldered man's muffled footsteps, the creaking of the ship's deck.

'What the hell are ye up to, sailor?'

He hid the paper, crumpling it behind his back. 'Nothing.'

'Don't lie to me, seaman. Give it to me.'

'Yes, sir.'

Tormod watched as Foster smoothed away the creases on the page, turning it over and over in his hand. Other than that he was Irish, he knew little about the officer – that he had a faint trace of an accent, said 'ye' instead of 'you', possessed an inability to pronounce the letters 'th' that was imitated by some of the crew. Nevertheless, there was a quiet sense of command in the way he dealt with the men, one that could also be seen in the steel-blue quality of his gaze as he concentrated on the drawing. His dark, closely-shaved head was bowed. He rubbed his chin, drawing attention to a faint red scar scratched across it.

'Yer name?' he said.

'Able Seaman Morrison.'

'First name?'

'Norman.' Tormod took a long time to squeeze out the word, his English name alien to his lips, accustomed to hearing it only in school.

Foster tapped the piece of paper on his fingers, the intensity of his stare now fully fixed on Tormod's face. 'Do ye have any more like this one?'

'One or two, sir.'

'In yer quarters?'

'Yes.'

'I thought this wasn't the first time you've spent time drawing while on duty. Ye can't be that unlucky.'

Tormod smiled and shrugged, aware that the officer wasn't that angry or annoyed with him. 'Most of them I just throw away when I'm finished.'

'Well, seaman, that's one thing that's going to change. I want ye to report with all of them to my quarters tomorrow at noon. After I have a squint of them, ye will also pick up better, proper paper instead of scraps like this.' He paused for a moment, a thin, pale smile crossing his lips. 'Continue with yer watch, Able Seaman Morrison.'

'Yes, sir.'

Tormod recalled how he had felt that moment he watched Foster stride down the deck, the lapels of his dark coat up around his neck. He noted so much about him: the dark hair shaved neat and even at the back of his neck, his blue eyes, the dimple on his cheek, even how clean the other man's fingers were. He doubted very much he had ever bent down low at the face of a peat-bank, shovelled out hay from a byre where the cattle had lain for the night. This man did not have a blacksmith for a father. Instead, Tormod imagined books, music, a painting or two on the walls. When he was in the Irishman's presence, he felt he was in the company of a man who did not belong to the same world he came from, where the rules that governed his behaviour were both uncertain and unknown.

He had been full of much the same mix of unease and anticipation on the day that, along with some of the other men from the Naval Reserve in the village, he had been called up to go to war. Part of him had dreaded the thought of the conflict. Another part longed for it. For once in his life, his father suffered no confusion. 'I'll tell you,' he declared as he put his scythe away that day, 'these politicians and soldiers have no idea what it's like to look after both a family and croft at my age. Otherwise, they'd have let you stay at home. They've no consideration whatsoever.'

His father's reaction strengthened him, allowing Tormod to see the arrival of his call-up papers as a release from the life he had known before. He had gone out that morning to clean the byre as usual. As he brushed away the last of the slurry, the greeny-brown liquid long settled in its drain, the broom between his fingers was transformed into a rifle. He imagined holding it and aiming it at all those who irritated and troubled him. He held it between his fingers, blasting away at the walls that had held and confined him for so long. His father. His new wife, Catriona. Even the village schoolmaster who had belted his fingers so often in the past.

'Pow! Pow! Pow! Rat-a-tat-tat!'

That resentment was with him as he went to Foster's room the next day. Knocking at the door, he wondered if his errand was a waste of time, part of that game of mischief and malice he had seen officers play so many times before. The quietness of Foster as he leafed through the pictures convinced him otherwise. 'Good, good,' he kept muttering.

'For an untrained hand and eye, these are very good.'

'Thank you, sir.'

'Oh, Morrison. Hold on. I'll get one of my journals for ye. My mother keeps sending them out. She thinks I'm the new Rembrandt or Michelangelo.'

He watched as Foster brought a blank notebook to him. His fingers marvelled at its linen cover, the texture of its pages as he took it in his hands. It felt rich and luxurious, different from any of the other sheets he had scribbled on before.

'And a couple of proper pencils too.'

He clasped them, too, in his hands. 'Thank you, sir.'

'Use them well, Morrison. Use them well. And make sure ye don't forget to come back and show me just how well you're using them. Remember that's part of the bargain too.'

'Yes, sir. Yes, sir.'

It took him a while, but he learned to master his nerves and materials. He would spend much of his free time out on the deck, sketching all that lay around him. Rocks and skerries, little spits of sand, the outline of a town on the horizon. Gannets, cormorants, gulls he could see winging their way across the ocean. He would store them away in his memory to bring them to life later on the page. There were the men, too, urging him to draw their faces as they stood before him on the deck or lounged about in their hammocks below.

'Come on, come on. Draw me. So I can send it off to my little darling back home. Who knows? It might even help keep me in mind the nights she's cold and lonely and tempted by the thought of our friendly butcher's little sausages going free a few doors away.'

He grinned as he gave in, trying to catch something of their features on the page. A glint in their eyes. A twist to their smile. Even a curl or cowlick that stayed in their hair, defying all attempts of the barber to train or trim it. Anything they could send home to their women to remind them not only of their appearance but also the spirit of the men they had known. Even the captain came to see him, sitting in his chair while Tormod sketched out his likeness on the paper.

Only one man did not approve. Macdermid, the man who was still with him at Inverness station, would glower at him whenever he sat with his pencil, tapping his coat pocket as though it were a pulpit edge or perhaps the cover of a Bible he had squeezed in there.

'His own iniquities shall take the wicked,' he would declare. 'He shall be holden with the cords of his sins.' There would be a reminder, too, of that earlier conversation. 'Remember. God never meant us to see our reflections, apart from within a murky pool or stream. He taught us to look within instead.'

Yet Tormod barely noticed the man's attitude – aware of it only as a reminder of his parents and the letters he had sometimes to force himself down to write. *My dear mother and father, All is fine here. We are spending most of our days quite peacefully at sea...* Instead, it was Foster's approval he sought most of all. The officer would sometimes hunker down beside him on the deck, nodding as he studied the sheet of paper.

'Good, Morrison. Very good. But you haven't quite got the perspective right there. Some more shading's needed here...' He would point, perhaps, to the foot of a rock or a bollard on the quayside. 'And here. And there. But on the whole, it's good. Very good.'

There were times, too, when Foster would bring out his pencil and paper, working alongside him. His eyes fixed on a gull perched on a ship's bow, he would rub the edge of his pencil-tip briskly across the page; stroking feathers into existence; etching out a webbed foot; hooking strong black lines to form a beak; a dark dot for the eye. Soon the bird – almost living, almost real – peered out from the page.

'What do you think of that then?'

'It's great. Much better than anything I could do.'

'At this stage, perhaps... But remember, I've had years of teaching and training. You have a much greater natural talent than I have. Yer shouldn't let it go to waste.'

Tormod's teeth clamped shut. 'Perhaps I've no choice.'

Foster smiled, the scar upon his chin glinting as he did so. 'Ah, seaman, we've all got choice. The only problem we have in life is recognising these moments when we do.'

His gaze low and serious, he spoke about his own life. He came from a place near Bandon in County Cork – 'one of the few parts of the south of Ireland where you can find a Protestant clutching a spade' – and had gone to Trinity College in Dublin to study architecture. It was a course he hadn't finished, joining up at a moment when 'the madness of the war had stirred men's blood and turned their heads'.

'And I don't know if I'll be going back there. Not now. Not to Ireland. The world is changing there. Another kind of madness taking hold, and I don't know if there's going to be a place for me and my kind when it does so. Any room for a man like me.'

He smiled as he gazed at the skyline, as if he were measuring the miles he might have to journey while he looked for a place he could settle down and stay.

'But, at least, it gives me an excuse to wander. Be like the wild geese that have flown so often from our shores. Who knows where I might end up? Spain, France. Amerikay.' He grinned at his own thoughts. 'And as long as I can draw, I have the means to settle anywhere. Just like you, seaman. Just like you. You're good enough to pick up work in a studio. Or even a street corner, if you're desperate.'

Seeing Foster again in his mind's eye, Tormod paused for a moment in his drawing of the Cameron statue. The Forres Fiddler was standing playing his instrument just a few yards away, blocking his view. He took in the shape of the man – his greatcoat, white beard and glengarry, his fiddle tucked below his chin – and thought he would be an interesting figure to draw. But not now. He still had the statue of the Highlander to complete. Digging into his pocket, he threw a coin in the fiddler's direction, hoping that if he did so, the man would move away quickly. He didn't have much time left. By next week, he would be back among the cows and sheep. Bringing them their winter straw. Hauling in their water. Cleaning out their shit.

Hell. He envied Foster. Tormod hadn't even the time to draw one of the buildings, in the way that the Irishman would have done. He'd sketch out in full, rich detail the Catholic churches which were found throughout Ireland, constructions like St Colman's Cathedral stretching out above the streets of Queenstown. Foster had gone there while on furlough, a few weeks after the *Lusitania* had been sunk. 'My father wanted to go there. Find out exactly what had happened. Speak to a few of his friends who lived in the town,' he explained. By the time they got there, bodies were no longer being carted through the streets of the town as they had been in the days that followed the sinking. Reporters and photographers had stopped their bustle through its hotels and boarding houses. And in its peace, while his father talked and gossiped, Foster had perched himself on a wall and drawn the vastness of that building. The towers and spires with their shadows. The stained glass windows with their shaded light.

There had been no such time for Tormod. Instead, he'd sweated as boxes were hoisted and carried, brought from the ship's hold to bring to the men garrisoned on a small island a few short miles away. And as he worked, he was always aware of the presence of the newly constructed building overlooking his labours. The sparkle of sun on its windows. The greyness of its stone walls. The thought and artistry that had gone into its creation.

It wasn't the only time he felt jealous of Foster. Even a glance at his hands could sometimes trigger his anger – soft and white instead of bruised and calloused, starred with sparks like his own fingers. It was clear he had never lifted a fork heavy with dung or the tangle of rotting seaweed in his existence. The feeling was at its worst when the officer showed him some watercolours of the sights he had come across during his time in Holland. An old brick house beside a bridge in Amsterdam. One of the royal palaces. A busy market town. A field full of flowers.

'Following in the footsteps of Rembrandt and Vermeer.

Just like my mother wants me to do.' Foster smiled.

Tormod grinned weakly, annoyed that he did not know who either man was. His irritation changed to curiosity, however, when Foster took out his next set of drawings.

'They're not the sort I'd ever show my mother,' he said apologetically. 'Not sure she'd quite approve.'

Guilt and excitement mingled as Tormod looked at them. It was almost as if he half-expected either Macdermid, his father or even Catriona to loom over his shoulder, comprehending all that he was studying with a glance. They were sketches of naked women: one sitting in a chair; another standing by a window; a third one perched upon a stool. His eye took it all in – the shapes and secrets that in island women were always covered by thick lengths of plaid or long stretches of skirt. The curve of thigh and breast. The strength of legs. The sweep of a shoulder. Even the richness of the hair that was normally concealed by a scarf in the women he had known in his youth.

'How would ye fancy drawing the likes of that?'

Tormod paused again in his sketching when he thought of that moment. He could hear all the uproar around him. In the hotel behind his back. Inside the railway station, where more men – back from their years of service – were gathering. Someone was shouting, 'It won't be long now, boys! It won't be long now!' Macdermid was standing at the edge of the crowd outside the railway office, grim and glowering as usual, while Jock was now singing a song that had traditionally been on the lips of women and was ringing out the chorus of *'Fear a' Bhàta'*, anticipating, perhaps, the voyage that was to come.

'Fhir a' bhàta, na hòro èile
Fhir a' bhàta, na hòro èile
Fhir a' bhàta, na hòro èile
Mo shoraidh slàn leat 's gach àit' an tèid thu.'

'O boatman and no one else,
O boatman and no one else,
O boatman and no one else,
My thoughts are with you wherever you go.'

He was barely aware of any of this. Instead, he recalled his own reaction to Foster's question, his mouth dry with shame and fear as he spoke.

'Aye... I'd love the chance to do the likes of that.'

He remembered, too, the night Foster had arranged for it all to happen. The rain spattering down on the streets of Rouen as they hurried, coming eventually to a darkened staircase lit only by the frail light of a gas-lamp. After climbing that, they had gone to a door where a grey-haired English woman, her face daubed with powder and lipstick, had greeted them. 'Ah, my artists... Messrs van Gogh and Constable, I presume – though no connection to His Majesty's, we hope.' She had led them inside to a room where a young, redheaded woman with a flush of freckles on her upper chest and arms had posed for them. Standing and sitting. Turning this way and that. Foster's voice commanding her in a way that his own would have quaked to do. 'A little bit more that way. No... That's too much.' His own heart hammering as he drew, amazed at the fact he was sitting there, sketching the outline of this woman's breasts and thighs, thinking, too, of the impossibility of doing this at home, where men like Macdermid might tut and disapprove even at the thought of nakedness in the marriage bed, where his new bride Catriona covered and hid herself from his gaze. ('It is all too easy, Tormod, to surrender to the animal that is in us all, to give in to the weaknesses of the flesh...') His pencil moving quickly and urgently across the page, aware that this might be his last chance to capture and record the mystery of the female body – with all its different shades and light.

It was Macdermid, too, who reminded him again of how those in the islands might respond to what he had done that day. One of his fellow crewmen had glimpsed the drawings in his possession as Tormod went through his belongings one day.

'Jesus. Let's see that. Let's see that!'

He had finally given in to him, watching as these drawings were passed from hand to hand among members of the crew, held up in the light as they tried to glimpse how much he had revealed of the woman's breasts, the secrets of the shadows down below.

'I wish I'd been there,' one joked. 'It wouldn't have been a pencil I was holding.'

'For all the lead you've got in it, it wouldn't have made much difference,' another yelled.

It was while they were in the middle of this that Macdermid arrived below deck. Tormod watched him as, his face stern and serious, he made his way towards his hammock. His Bible was lying there. His hand clutched it moments before he swung his body up, stretching out its length. His fingers leafed through the book's pages. His lips moved, muttering its words. Tormod could even imagine hearing them echoing around the ship.

'*Why wilt thou, my son, be ravished with a strange woman and embrace the bosom of a stranger?*'

And then one of the crewmen's voices broke the silence. 'Hey, holy man! Do you want to see the pictures the other man from the isles has drawn?'

He saw Macdermid's gaze shift round – a brief squint at the picture brandished between the sailor's hands followed by a long, deploring stare in his direction. The Harrisman's mouth twisted with its certainties.

'Have you fallen so low, Morrison?'

Tormod looked up once again at Macdermid, who was still standing in front of the railway office, exchanging words with some like-minded islander desperate, too, to return to his home after the war. Their faces dark and thunderous, Tormod could easily imagine their pious whispers, the swapping of verse and text that was occurring. Each glance would contain a prediction of what might happen one day to men like him, their souls sullied by contact with the outside world. ('*He shall die without instruction; and in the greatness of his folly he shall go astray.*') By the time they reached the shores of Stornoway, their gaze would become even sharper and more acute, their voices louder and more confident, echoing within a community that had been fashioned in their own image.

It was all too easy for Tormod to imagine how he would feel when he arrived there. Surrounded by these men and their voices. Dominated by his father or, later, when the old man finally gave in to the force of illness or death, by his marriage to a woman whose every thought and movement was confined by some minister's narrow understanding of the Bible, the tightness of her plaid and length of her skirt. Following the haunches of cattle making their way home from the croft. The flicking of their tails. Midges. The swish of udders. Their smell of milk and motherhood. Their stink of shit. The spray of sparks hammered out on an anvil. All of that would leave him as lifeless as the statue he had just finished drawing. Cameron of Lochiel with his dead eyes watching the men gathering at the station, returning after their sacrifice, eager for their homes.

It was then he remembered some of Foster's earliest words on the ship. *You're good enough to pick up work in a studio. Or even a street corner, if you're desperate.* It was this memory that made him ponder about what to do. He could go back only for a short time and then he would sail from its shores. The moment he became a civilian again, he would pack his bags and leave.

There was nothing he wanted in that place.

Nothing whatsoever for him.

1936

It was a moment that possessed an element of a miracle.

Or at least that was my grandma's view when she heard of what happened in our classroom that day. Her hands, worn and rubbed, immediately clasped together. Her mouth trembled and blurred.

'Oh Lord, you have heard what the boy has talked to us about, of a voice coming all the way from London to tell us of what is happening in places far away from this island. Let us be glad and grateful that the news they talk of is reaching us here upon this shore. We are grateful for the miracles you are providing us with, how it is changing the world around us, making our lives better than they were…'

She carried on for a while, her voice reaching the intensity it sometimes possessed when she was in the byre, as if she hoped that her prayers and wishes might reach her relatives over the moor in North Tolsta, as if she wanted them to be aware that she was thinking of them, too, and not just those whom she lived alongside, her words imitating the airwaves she praised.

The headteacher, Roderick MacAskill, had a very different reaction to all of that. He appeared in class one day with a box in his arms. His brown eyes gleaming, he placed it on the front desk, taking out its contents. One by one, they appeared: a long-life Vidor battery, a wooden box with the wording 'Instructions for using the Revophone Crystal Set' scrolled upon it, a set of earphones attached. As they came out, they were accompanied by gasps of awe and wonder from the pupils who looked out at him.

'What is it?' some boy asked.

'It's a wireless,' I answered, an expert because of my years in Glasgow. 'It tells people what's happening in the world.'

'Good,' MacAskill declared, dimples appearing as he grinned. He swept a hand back over his balding head, once dark but now slowly giving way to grey. 'I bought it for our home. There's someone there who feels left out if she doesn't know what's going on out there.'

We all knew to whom he was referring. One of the boys near me even whispered 'Elizabeth' to his neighbour, in what he imagined was a posh English accent. A moment or two later and there were a string of half-muffled giggles. 'Elizabeth,' someone else echoed.

He raised a finger to his lips before he spoke next, making sure the the room was in silence. A strange series of words came to his mouth as he turned two switches with his hands, dialling them round and round. 'Friends, Romans and Islesmen. I come to bury the past and not to praise it. The evil that men do lives after them. The good is oft interred with their bones.'

After that, the remainder of the marvel occurred. A whistling noise as the wireless was tuned. A set of pips at intervals of one second. Finally, there was another voice in that classroom, one that sounded remarkably English, the hushed and authoritative tones of God.

'This is the BBC Home Service. Here is the News and this is Alvar Lidell reading it…'

There was a gasp, a sigh of astonishment.

A few moments later, the toll of words began.

'The English-born aviator, Beryl Markham, has become the first woman to undertake the East–West transatlantic flight, flying from Abingdon-on-Thames in Berkshire to Cape Breton Island, Nova Scotia. In the ongoing civil war in Spain, after heavy fighting, the Basque city of Irún, near the French border, has been taken by the Nationalists under General Mola. Francisco Largo Caballero has also been appointed as Prime Minister and Minister of War for the Spanish government…'

I glanced over at my sister, wondering how she was taking it all in. She looked distant as ever, eyes wide and austere as moons. A week or so before, she had slipped away through the school gates and across the croftland of North Dell, skulking behind haystacks, making her way through herds of cattle, flocks of sheep. Across the river and into South Dell, dodging Druim Fraoich and any ghost that might be hiding there, she kept on going till she reached our croft, crouching behind the walls of the new white houses, built after the Great War, and the thatched blackhouses that had stood there for years, fields stretched out behind them.

Grandad found her among the horses, going there when one of the older pupils arrived to tell those in the household that Rachel had disappeared. When he discovered her, he stretched out his hands and lifted her on the back of an old grey mare, the one they called Murdag. Holding her reins, they trotted together in the direction of the school. When he reached there, he raised her from the horse once again, speaking quietly and firmly to her.

'Promise you'll stay in school from now on.'

She nodded in response.

'After all, you don't want to get your old grandad in trouble.'

Again, the quiet smile, the nod of the head.

He took her with him into the school. 'There'll be no more trouble, Mr MacAskill. She'll be with you from now on.'

This time, it was Mr MacAskill's turn to nod, ushering her into the building.

Yet even when she was in the classroom, it was as if she was barely aware of all that was taking place, unreachable by words, looks and gestures. The headmaster had even gone so far as to ask me about her one day: 'Does she ever talk at all?'

I shook my head. 'No. Not really.'

'Do you think it might be the effect of other children speaking Gaelic around her?'

'No.'

'What about the way your grandad and grandma speak Gaelic? Do you think that might be having an effect?'

'No. I don't think so.'

'She doesn't miss English then? Not as part of her world?'

'No. I don't think so.'

I am aware that, nowadays, MacAskill might have read something or even spoken to a local doctor. He could have discovered what I found out many years later, that 'selective mutism' is experienced by very few people, but is most common in girls and children who are learning a second language, especially those who have travelled from one country to another. In some ways, that would have been the case with many of my classmates. They had to make a similar journey, moving from houses where Gaelic was just about the only tongue spoken to a school in which there was little but English, where they had to answer questions like, 'What is Leicester famous for?' or, '*What is sanctification?*' (*Sanctification is the work of God's free grace whereby we are renewed in the whole man after the image of God...*) Sometimes they stammered when they did this, compelled to master long and complex words in a language where they had little more than the basics, its shapes unfamiliar to both lip and tongue. When they did this well, MacAskill would clap his hands and smile broadly.

'Well done. A language fit for princes now flows from the mouth of a peasant.'

Yet it must have been stranger still for us – to move from a tenement flat to a blackhouse, from a city to a croft, our lives lifted up and lowered down to a small village on an island. If MacAskill had questioned me further, he might have gained some information about this. However, he simply sighed and walked away, as if he was defeated by my first response, my inability to admit that the language surrounding her was part of the problem, isolating and preventing her from speaking to others. Yet the truth was that it wasn't that particular issue which walled her from others. The one time I managed to question her about her silence, she answered in a quiet, whistling voice, one that in no way resembled her own:

'I miss my mum.'

I said I did so too, frightened to admit even to myself that my memory of her – and my dad – was fading. I could recall my father's beery breath as he spoke of Willie Mills and Matt Armstrong, his mat of brown hair, the redness of his complexion. My mother was fainter still – to the extent that when I see her nowadays, I no longer picture *her*. Instead, my grandad's young wife comes to mind, with her dark curls, the roundness of her face, the way she was drawn in his journals. As for the sound of my mother's voice, I could no longer recall it at all.

Tormod's Journals

December 1918

Grey land skidded by. The only chips in its murky half-light were made by an occasional houselight or the water of a nearby loch swishing like the slow rhythm of an axe as it lapped towards the land's edge. The train wheels cast out small blue-white sparks. The engine churned curls of black smoke that were all too familiar to him. Tormod had seen the same darkness clouding the funnels of the vessels on which he had travelled again and again over the last few years – the *Lochness, Aboukir, Glengarry.* There were days when he had spat into the sea or the palm of his hand and seen that the same stain clouded his insides, his throat, the working of his chest, his stomach, as if the smoke and heat of his father's forge had haunted him throughout his travels, reminding him constantly of where he had to return after these years were over. He shook the thought from his head and looked outside as the train passed through Contin, Conon Bridge, Strathpeffer, the shadow of a forest, mountain, a row of houses, a stone wall rising to meet the rail like the boundary of a prison. Each one identical to him in his current mood. The clouds were lowering around him. A smattering of rain dotted the carriage window, obscuring even the tight limits of his view.

He felt once again as if his life was narrowing down.

Colour vanishing from his existence along with daylight.

That there were still miles to go before his journey would be over.

He half-listened to the conversations going on around him. They spun and spun, looping in continual circles. At one moment, they seemed to be about what the men had experienced in the war. The next, they were talking about their future lives, back on the island. For a couple of them, their two lives seemed to blur and mingle. There was a man called Roddy Murray who had spent much of the war on the *Canopus*, one of the few ships in the Navy that never really sailed.

'I've been stuck for the last few years in Port Stanley in the Falkland Isles, looking at penguins, seals and sea lions, a damn whale or two. The boat was a little bit like us – fixed into the shoreline in the one place, its guns trained on the open sea, empty oil barrels used as mines. Just as well I was well used to eating fish and manky sheep, as that was all we ever got morning, noon and night. Just enough to keep us on the go painting the boat the same shade as the moor all around us. Seemed to be all we did most days, cloud and camouflage our lives. Try to be unseen and unnoticed.'

A man called John Murdo laughed. He had spent much of his time in Scapa Flow in Orkney. He had been there in 1916 at the end of May, when the Grand Fleet set out in all its grey glory for Jutland. He recalled what it had been like that evening, the racket that took place as the stokers sweated in the boiler room for hours to make sure the ships were right and ready for the voyage. There was the hum of the draught

fans from the grey ships, the guns and searchlights being
checked, their beams glowing through the thick clouds of
smoke covering the waters, the funnels belching black.

'...And then there were the bloody bugles, the sound of
orders being shouted, the gangways being hoisted. A few
hours after that and they were on their way, following the
minesweepers out of those waters on their way to what the
officers called *Der Tag, an latha mòr*, the big day of battle.
And we were back to something that wasn't all that different
from where we came from. Fields of hay, oats and barley.
Crops of potatoes. Cattle. Horses. Sheep.'

'And what were the sheep like?' Roddy Murray asked.
'Scraggy like the ones I saw in Port Stanley?'

'Oh, no,' John Murdo laughed. 'They were fine animals.
Fat and strong. All grazing on the fine fields near Scapa.'

'Ours will be like that after the war,' Roddy Murray said.
'A big improvement on what we have now.'

'How?'

'Well, the Government has promised land for all those
who signed up. The farms in places like Melbost, Galson and
Gress to be broken up and given to the people of the island.
It'll give people the chance of a fresh beginning, a new way
of life.'

Tormod again recalled the day he had first heard that
promise – how, from all parts of the parish, men and women
crammed the kirk, squashed together on the pews, sitting
tight, shoulder to shoulder, lined up on the floor before
the pulpit and between the aisles. He had been with his
neighbours Iain Help and his brothers, Aoghnas Thuathain
and Dòmhnall Stufain, as Macdougall the minister preached

to them, offering up a vision of a better, fairer world if the men of the district signed their names and took up arms, telling of how the authorities had 'promised to give each man land if they sign up to serve the King in this war. Acres for them to plough and harvest. Farms will be broken up to provide this. Land for sheep and cattle to graze. Soil in which crops can be planted.'

He had felt bedazzled that day – not for his own sake but because of the younger men of the district who wanted to build new foundations for their lives. They needed to dream of an existence other than the penury they had always suffered. He sensed how the minister's words seared deep in them, how they would remember this strange sermon for years to come, wherever they travelled in the world.

'Write down your names,' the minister had continued. 'Take up the King's shilling. It will bring the people of this island not only security but a sense of justice and fairness, a feeling that they are involved in the creation of another, better world.'

Tormod wasn't so sure about that now. He wasn't certain that the landscape he knew so well could resurrect itself in the way some of these men appeared to believe might happen. These men didn't have the energy for that. There would be too many ghosts and skeletons on the island. The dead, the crippled, the wounded – some of them might not have been able to make their way home, but they were present in its moors and shoreline, fields and seas just the same, carcasses that lay like the corpses of those sheep that sometimes die in a bog or near a loch, rotten and unburied. He knew that their presence would have their effect on him each time he walked through South Dell. He would think of those that were gone from particular houses and croftlands, the men he would never see again or those who were damaged – whether in mind or soul – by the war. Could a place like that rise and resurrect itself, acquire new flesh for the bareness of its land, resuscitate a community which had all but gone? He wasn't sure that could happen. Not even if crops were planted on bare land, sheep and cattle sent out to graze on fields that young men had just gained for themselves. Not even if they broke down old farm-walls and built new homes where a factor's house had once stood, waved red flags where they had trampled down old boundaries.

He didn't say anything about that, kept quiet and listened. There was a young man called Charlie, who had spoken earlier when the train was just leaving Inverness. A red-haired, freckled fellow from the village of Carloway, he had talked about how much he loved the machines he had seen and heard during his time away. Placing a hand on the compartment window, he muttered about how the noise of the train was like a heartbeat – 'Sha-room, sha-room, sha-room, clickety-clack, clickety-clack, clickety-clack' – to him.

'It keeps me alive,' he said. 'It's as if my heart should have been a piston in a steam engine.'

They laughed, grinning even more when he spoke with excitement about the journey he had taken over the last few days after he had disembarked in Birkenhead.

'I'll tell you, I was really worried when I got to the Scottish border. I thought it would be as if we were travelling up a cliff, hauling and chuntering all the way. But it was nothing like that. I hardly even noticed the difference for miles.'

'You do now,' Tormod said, grinning.

'Aye. Nothing but rocks and moorland. Acres that aren't even worth the use of a plough. It's so up and down it makes me think I'm still at sea.'

Tormod looked across at Roddy Murray. He was talking of the new land he would obtain when they broke up the farm at Gress, dug deep for their new homes within its boundaries, built up walls and gathered thatch from its open acres.

'I'm looking forward to taking Asquith there.' Roddy smiled. 'See him graze near the factor's house.'

'What?'

'Our horse.'

'You mean you called the poor beast after a politician?'

'Aye. He talks a lot more sense than one. His dung is of greater use too.'

'You shouldn't be paying the creature an insult like that,' Tormod said. 'No horse should be called after a politician. They're far too noble for that.'

'There won't be many of them left soon,' Charlie interjected.

'What?

'The machine will be taking over, churning up fields like the armoured tank. Sewing and harvesting. Carrying us for miles and miles.'

Tormod bridled, thinking of the wonder of the animal he loved. Pegasus. Buraq. The creature who had lifted his spirits when he felt lonely and bereft at sea. A quick thought of its strength and power flashed through his head, the countless sketches he had made of its beauty when he found moments of peace on the *Glengarry*.

'You sure?' he said. 'I doubt it. The land's too poor to pay for machines.'

'The sea will help us do that. The ling and herring. That's just one more reason why we'll need trains on the island, lorries and not horse and cart. Otherwise, we might as well pack up and go to other places.'

'You're thinking of doing that?' Tormod asked.

'Aye. And I won't be alone. A lot of us are restless. Now that we've seen the rest of the world, we won't want to go back to cold potatoes and Sunday worship. No indeed.'

For all that he could hear songs being bellowed in a nearby carriage, a chorus or two of 'Eilean Fraoich', the Lewis anthem, Tormod nodded. There was some truth in his words. Though they might now be singing about the joys of going back to the island, it would not be long before there would be another chorus and melody on their lips. English songs like those that Jockie had changed and adapted, making his own.

'Iain Murdo, won't you please come home?'

'Pack up your troubles in an old *cailleach's* scarf.'

Songs about the joys of a new life in Canada or the USA.

About working in a factory or shipyard in Glasgow.

About escaping the tightness of the world where they lived.

1936

'Tell your dad about the wireless.'

I looked across at Grandad on the other side of the table.

'Write him a letter. Let him know that this place isn't as backward as a man from the mainland might think it is. Tell him we've even got a wireless in the classroom. Tell him we even know all about Stanley Baldwin in this place.'

'You sure?'

'Aye. He'd love to get a letter from you.'

And that was how I wrote my first ever letter, sitting there with a pencil and paper at the table, scratching out a message as best I could.

Dearest Daddy,

I am writing to tell you all the news from here. The school got a radio the other day. A voice came on to tell us all about Stanley Baldwin and some lady who managed to fly from somewhere near London to Canada. She may even have flown over the island but nobody noticed. All Great-Uncle Calum says is that he noticed the seagulls were in some state that day. They probably don't like men and women being in the sky.

*Everyone here is well. Even the old horse Fingal
that Grandad is looking after. He keeps stuffing her
with hay. Rachel is as quiet as ever. She never says
anything much but sends you her love. As for Grandad,
Grandma and Great-Uncle Calum, they are in their
usual. Waking and complaining as usual, as they
always say. They are helping me to get to know the
village. For all that some of the people here are grumpy,
they always talk to you, though I cannot always make
sense of what they say. That's not just because they
speak the Gaelic but because they have an awful habit
of talking too fast...*

'Ask him about money,' I heard Grandma whisper.

'No,' Grandad muttered. 'I won't be getting the child to do that.'

'But why not? Most fathers would pay an allotment to those who are looking after their children. Does he think they're fed on air?'

'I don't imagine he's thinking too much at the moment, Catriona. He's probably still grieving.'

'You give him too much credit. You know only too well what kind of man he is.'

'Catriona... The boy may be listening.'

I pretended I wasn't, continuing to scribble on that page. At the same time, I was remembering how we had lived together in our flat in Glasgow. Apart from the height of the ceiling, giddy and inaccessible above my head, the place was narrow and confined – one bedroom where my mother and father had slept, Rachel in her own tiny bed at their feet, a scullery. I slept in a box-bed in the sitting room which also served as the kitchen; the toilet was in the yard behind the tenement. From the landing outside, voices would sometimes seep in. A quarrel between a mother and a child. A drunken neighbour stumbling home. Angry words being exchanged between a husband and wife. A baby crying.

We contributed our share of noises too. Occasionally Rachel and I would argue. Over the month or so before her death, my mother would cough, a loud, hacking sound that seemed far too powerful for such a frail wisp of an individual. There would be the sheen of sweat on her features, her hair pasted back against her scalp and forehead. 'Och, och,' she would say in that Hebridean accent of hers which was so distinctive when people heard it in these streets. 'Is there no end to this?' Sometimes, though I was barely aware of this, there was the spit and hiss of blood, a red stain left in either hand or handkerchief, a cry of sorrow and distress. I shut my ears to all of this, preferring instead to be soothed by my father's talk of his early life in Aberdeen.

'Ye see a lot more of the sea than around here, Alasdair. It's not just a wee-bit river like the one they're so proud of in these parts. Not at all. When I was a bairn, me and the lads used to walk out all the way to the Torry Battery, see where the auld guns used to be. We'd gae oot too to da lighthouse at Girdle Ness, watching the lichts o' ships oot in da North Sea, the fishing boats coming in frae the fierce storms that sometimes lashed the place. Sometimes we'd stroll in the direction of the Beach and the Bathing Station, looking at a' that was going on there. That was a different world, a different kind of skirling going on aroond there.'

His eyes would water when he spoke of these places, mentioning locations that sounded a little like the way Stornoway, too, might have been at one time – streets filled with fish-boxes and men hauling fish out from boats tied at the harbour, seagulls – or 'scurries' as Dad called them – filling the skies with their clamour.

'These beggars would snatch a sandwich out of yer han' if ye didnae gang canny.'

His gaze would become even more bleary still as he continued, that familiar reek lacing his breath. He would mention places like Duthie Park and the old Winter Gardens – 'where the snobs hang out' – as his arm drooped, no longer tight and wrapped around my shoulder. Eventually, after a brief time wandering the length of Union Street with its towers and tall buildings, shops and stores, he would arrive at his final destination – the little terraced house near the harbour where his family had grown up.

'Bastards. They're no longer talking tae me. Not after that day in court. Ma ain fowk. They turned their backs on me.'

He would surrender to gloom and moodiness for a moment, his lips pursing, his eyes glazed. A few moments later, he shook himself out of this state. Seeking to restore some cheer to himself, he forced a thin smile, his accent becoming more dense and impenetrable with drink.

'But for a' that, Ah tell ye George Cruickshank has nae lack i' freens in yon city. Nae doot aboot 'at. If ah gid back aire, aire'd be fowk aroon tae help me cope an' support me. Ah can rest assured aboot 'at.'

He nodded to himself, looking at the calendar that was fixed to the scullery door with its picture of Union Street and all its high towers, as if merely saying these words had provided him with a certainty that was absent from any other part of his life.

Tormod's Journals

December 1918

Tormod had seen his fellow villager Finlay when their journey halted for a while at Garve. A few of the men scrambled out there, desperate to do their toilet somewhere other than the one on the train with its heady stink of piss and shit. It was then that the fair-haired sailor had spotted his neighbour sitting in that crammed apartment. His hand outstretched, his voice loud in greeting, he had squeezed in beside Tormod, shifting into an empty seat caused by Charlie from the village of Carloway moving elsewhere.

'It's great to see a fellow Daileach. One of my fellow villagers. I was beginning to think there were none of you around.'

And then the intrusion began, an end to the isolation that Tormod had guarded since he arrived at Inverness station, knowing there would be precious little of it in existence when he arrived at his destination. South Dell would disturb both his and everybody else's business as it had done again and again throughout his years.

He had a good idea, too, how it would happen, conscious that Finlay was like his brother Roddy in his fondness for postcards. Their mother had a fine collection of the ones his sibling had sent to her on his travels. She was the one who would harass anyone who hung around too long near her home, pressing one on them, pointing out that Roddy had visited them on his travels. The Golden Gate Bridge. Yellowstone National Park. That one with the branches of a giant tree. ('If you look closely, you'll find someone in there. Trapped among the leaves.') Not unlike the tree that had washed up in Dìobadal on the other side of the island, its roots torn from the earth by a storm that had swept across the coastline of Sutherland, carried away on tides and currents, a little like the men who surrounded them in the compartments of the train.

Finlay reached into a pocket for his own collection of postcards.

They featured some of the places he had encountered in his travels – George Square in Glasgow, the Royal Liver Building on the waterfront at Liverpool, the Town Hall at Birkenhead. And then there were the other locations he had sailed to over the years. Names forgotten or perhaps never even known, their existence was noted in hurried descriptions he had scribbled in notes tucked into his pocket during the times his ship, the *Glasgow*, was tied up there.

Off the coast of South America, this one is the largest of a number of volcanic islands. It is dominated by three volcanic peaks, all sleeping, as well as a number of lower foothills. Not many people live here.

This is a small green island, a place of low hills that the rain – just like home – always washes. The winters, too, are almost as cold as our own. It even has a rocky coastline. If it wasn't for the way it's greener and possesses more trees than Lewis, it would be easy to think I was at home.

A small island, there is not much there except rocks. Despite this, a few families live there. This must be because of the fishing in its waters.

There were also other pictures in his pocket. One was of Tirpitz the pig. This round-bellied creature had been on the *Dresden* when it was sunk. One of the other crewmen had nearly drowned taking it on board the *Glasgow*, the creature's girth and panic hard to wrestle with as it tried to swim away from the wreckage of the German ship. After they had done this, the crew took photographs of it, standing still behind the camera when they decked it out with a spiked helmet on its head, a notice with the words 'Kaiser Bill' swinging below its neck. Sometimes they would even go further than that, knotting a bell around it which tinkled wherever it waddled up and down the deck.

And then there were the photographs of the other marvellous creations he had seen on his travels. A man dressed as a mermaid when he crossed the equator for the first time, King Neptune standing by his side. A half-upright elephant seal on the shoreline in the Falklands – like his brother's photograph of 'JUMBO THE ELEPHANT – THE TOWERING MONARCH OF HIS MIGHTY RACE' in the States. The strange penguins too, with wisps of yellow and black feathers on their heads, swaggering up and down a rock-strewn beach.

'I've heard you were good at drawing,' Finlay said.

'Who told you that?'

'Oh, everybody. Someone said you were as good as Michelangelo or even that fellow, Vincent van Gogh.'

Tormod looked up, rubbing sleep from his eyes, wondering partly at how much his skills had been exaggerated or, even more, how his fellow villagers had even heard of these names. Through the window, he could see the lights on in a big house someone said was called Achanalt, the home of the family of the late Sir Arthur Bignold, who had been the MP for Wick before the war. It occurred to him that its occupants might be sitting there worrying about some of the promises that had been made at the start of the conflict, how those who volunteered were to be given land in the places like these, the emptiness of the West Highlands. The lights of the railway carriage glinted on the surface of Loch a' Chroisg, appearing and vanishing, a little – Tormod suspected – like the vows that had been made by politicians and ministers some four or more years before, old words once said and now forgotten.

'I wonder if you could help me,' Finlay said, whispering to him.

'I can try.'

'I need to get a drawing of my girlfriend. It would be great to take one home with me.'

'Of course. I'll do my best.'

'It's just that I've heard you're very good at drawing women. Some of the men have been talking about that.'

Tormod blushed, his eyes narrowing as they settled on Macdermid. He wondered how much the Harrisman had told the other libertymen about how Foster had arranged to find women to allow him to draw.

'Is this girlfriend of yours from Dell?' he said.

'No. No. No.'

'Cross? Swainbost? Eoropie?' he said, reeling off the names of villages he knew were close at hand.

'No,' Finlay smiled. 'A little farther away than that.'

'Tolsta? Gress? Across the moor?'

Finlay laughed, as if he found the notion of these names even dafter than the ones mentioned before. 'No. Farther, much farther than that.'

'Where then?'

Finlay took out an envelope filled with photographs from his pocket, spreading them outwards in his fingers like a fan. The top one was of a dark, winsome woman with short black hair decorated by a white ribbon, a mouth smothered by lipstick, and a look of perpetual surprise in her eyes. A necklace sparkled and looped around her throat.

Tormod could not suppress a laugh. 'Who on earth is she?' he asked.

'Her name is Alice Brady.'

He grinned again, thinking of this man's boldness in bringing such beauty to a place like South Dell. Even bell-heather and bog-heather trembled there in the face of storms, far less something or someone as fragile and precious as this. He looked at the other pictures, her identity becoming clearer as he did so. They showed the same woman in a number of cinema posters; *Miss Petticoats, The Gilded Cage,* as Mimi in *La Bohème* (*Surprisingly Magnificent – Gorgeously Picturesque – Amazingly Beautiful*), *A Maid of Belgium* (*What War Did To One Girl Who Stood In Its Path.*)

'Have you met her?' Tormod said.

'Oh, no…'

'Asked her parents for her hand in marriage?'

'No. No. Of course not. I've just seen her in the flicks.'

'You really think she'll settle down well in South Dell?'

'Of course,' Finlay laughed. 'Can't you just imagine her with all the widows and spinsters there? It might give them all a few ideas.'

'I don't think she'll be alone in finding it hard to settle down there,' he said, looking round at his fellow passengers. Some of them seemed tired and haggard, exhausted through their years at war. Others were restless, speaking of the strips of land they were going to obtain now that the conflict was over. Some, like him, felt in two minds about going back to the island. They talked among themselves about the places they had been, valuing each voyage for the freedom it had given them rather than the tight confinement of their island.

'I went to Halifax in Nova Scotia. Our ship sailed there. Loads of elbow room to be found.'

'There's no place I saw quite like New Zealand. Really fancy the thought of going back there again.'

'Or the States… You can build a new life for yourself there.'

But the most worrying of all were the men who stayed silent. They looked as if they had travelled distances that no love, affection or words could ever help them cross over once again.

1992

Sometimes, writing about my grandfather's journals is not the most complicated aspect about completing this task. This is not to say that it is easy to do any of that. As I have noted before, there are moments when his writing is difficult to follow, his prose consisting of a strange concoction of old-fashioned grace and awkwardness, one perhaps caused by his inability to even think in English on occasion, far less write in it. And so I struggle to comprehend it, far less to translate it into a modern idiom that today's readers might find easy to understand. It is a process that feels like a betrayal, a denial of the purpose he sought for it, one at which I can only guess. Even the fact that his words are not written in Gaelic – a language I have long lost – adds to the sense of falsity I sometimes perceive within those pages.

There is also another kind of distance that yawns up between us. He was a man born before the beginning of the twentieth century. I am an individual whose existence has been mainly in its latter half. His life was predominantly rural; his focus often fixed upon the horse, that creature which he loved. My existence has been largely urban. Most of my childhood and teenage years in Aberdeen. Much of my adult life in Glasgow. Dealing with my son, Jamie, over the last few years, a young man much more like my father than my grandfather or me, spending all his money on drink, drifting through his days. As a result, there are moments when my eyes glaze and I turn away from my grandfather's writings. There was one occasion, for instance, when he wrote a great deal about a horse they called Samson and how his aversion to flies and midges made him useless for much of the summer months. Insect bites made his hide come out in welts and small cuts, no matter how people sought to protect them. For this reason, my great-grandfather, Tormod's father, wanted the creature dead.

'A waste of hay and fodder,' he'd declared.

The fury with which my grandfather writes about this renders almost every word illegible. You can sense the manner in which he grips his pen, the anger with which he almost scores each word through the page.

The horse should not have been slaughtered, he wrote. *Not for him. Not for anything.*

Yet for all the difficulties I have in bringing my grandfather to life on the sheets of paper on which I write, there are others who are far more complex and problematic. One of them is myself as a child; those years as distant from me as my grandfather with all the sombre sobriety he possessed at that time, hammering wheels and horseshoes with tools and techniques I cannot identify or name. I am no longer the boy I was back then, hiding my sense of grief and loss with meaningless chatter, endless questions about the world in which I had landed.

'Why isn't there a city here? Why do a few people still have their fires in the middle of their households? Why do they still speak Gaelic in this place?'

And I remember both my Great-Uncle Calum and my grandfather's endless patience with these questions, even the few words of prayer my grandmother uttered before risking a reply, and I wonder if I would have the same patience if something similar happened today, if any of my family died and I was forced to look after their children. Would I have the strength and forbearance that they showed to me?

1936

Outside the pages of the journals, which take all my waking hours to sift and work through, there is also the one who was the greatest mystery of all during that time, the individual who, more even than me, never got over her loss and sorrow during her early years. Rachel was the one who often cried and kicked in the middle of the night during that time. As a young boy, it was easy for me to forget the torment she was suffering, especially in the way she struggled to cope with the gap our mother had once filled in our lives, our father's absence, even the lack of an envelope containing a money order to support us while we were living on the island, the sense of anger and betrayal we both felt.

I shared a box-bed with her, head to toe, and often I would wake in the darkness with my chest or stomach pummelled by a lunge of her feet, delivering a series of blows in my direction. I winced each time she kicked me but tried my best not to cry out. I knew that she was asleep. I had a good idea, too, what she might be dreaming about, her thoughts revealed to me on one of the few occasions she spoke at that time of her life.

'Will you pray? Like Mammy?'

I knew exactly what she meant. Not like Grandma with her long litany of prayer. Or even the Minister and Church elders who sometimes came to visit our house, bowing their heads for an eternity as though all the burdens of that eternity were weighing and grinding them down. Just the few words our mother used to say. Words I echoed in the darkness.

> *'Now I lay me down to sleep,*
> *I pray the Lord my soul to keep,*
> *His Love to guard me through the night,*
> *And wake me in the morning's light.'*

'Thank you,' she mouthed.

And then she was asleep.

But I was the one awake, recalling the last year or two of our lives in Glasgow. There was a great deal I missed from my time there. The way the light broke in through the faded red curtains into the room, showing all that surrounded me. There was the clock on the mantelpiece, the old mirror that hung above it, the picture of Union Street bright with sunlight on the scullery door. Before the fire was the settee where my dad sat and talked most of the night. I could sniff the air, smelling his presence, the stink of tobacco deep in every crook and corner of the room, while I listened out for familiar sounds. The ticking of the clock. The voices of people on the street outside. The bark of my mother's cough.

Things grew worse when that became silent. Instead, I heard other people speaking. My mother's friend Seonag, who had been working with her in service in Kersland Street once upon a time, came to help us for a short while, until she gave birth to the child she was carrying. After that, she had her own concerns. And then there was Dad's aunt, Peg, the woman from Aberdeen who had first obtained work for Dad in Glasgow. She occasionally visited us, sniffing at the mess around us, cajoling and lecturing my father.

'Come on, son. You cannae let this get you down. You've got bairns to care for, mouths to feed. They are your responsibility and you've got to get off your bum and look after them.'

'If Ah was back at home, that wad be easy.'

'Well, wha scuppered that one?' Peg would ask. 'It's your own fault that you've ended up in these parts. If you hadn't taken that money, you wouldn't have landed here. Even then you should be counting your blessings that you have any job at all.'

'Sssshhhh…' Dad gestured towards me as I lay pretending to be asleep in bed.

'Well, stop your whining, son, and luik to yer bairns. You're part of the reason that they're here and it's your joab tae care for them.'

Yet the whining didn't stop. There were hours when I would be drawing at the kitchen table and he would sit alone on the settee, gazing at the embers of the fire, throwing cigarette butts – one after the other – into the ash-filled grate. His eyes fixed and glazed, he would mumble over and over again, going over his lost battles, his life in Aberdeen.

'Christ, Ah miss so much about my life there… The fishmarket at the end of the central pier. The ice cream parlours. The Winter Gardens with all their green. Jesus. Ah can e'en smell these places now. As if they're part of my skin.'

I woke once with his ramblings. He stretched out to hold me, his arm sprawled across the tweed blanket my mother had brought down from the island, the one that her own father or mother might have made, given to her that day she went into service in the city.

'Sorry, son. Ah didnae mean to wake you. Just that your poor dad gets so lonely sometimes he blabbers awa' tae himsel'. He misses yer ma somethin' awful. He has tae ha'e a yarn with himself instead. Sorry for waking you. Sorry. Sorry.'

Even I – child though I was – could see that it was all too much for him. He couldn't cope with any of it. In that way, he shared some of the feelings that my grandad must have experienced waiting on the pier for us at Stornoway harbour just a short time later. Grandad must have looked down at his wrinkled hands, the little blue stars that sparked on his skin, and wondered how both he and his wife would cope with the young boy and girl that were about to enter their home, one that already had a semi-cripple within its walls, one the two of them had to help dress and feed. He must have shaken and shuddered with a similar sense of desolation to the one that afflicted him not far away from there during the early hours of 1919, watching many of those who had sailed on that ship with him disappear forever below the waves.

Tormod's Journals

December 1918

Tormod heard the telegram operator in Kyle of Lochalsh laughing as she scribbled the words the men wanted to send when they arrived at the post office in the port.

'It makes such a change,' she kept saying. 'It makes such a wonderful change.'

He knew exactly what she meant. For so long, people had feared the arrival of the telegram man in the village. He normally carried bad news in his satchel. The death of a son in the conflict. The loss of a husband, nephew, uncle. There was one day in May a few years before when bad news had weighed particularly heavy. It was the news of nine deaths in the parish, slowing the poor man's steps as he moved from one household to the next, conscious of the terrible burden he was carrying. Tormod could even recall the names and the places where they had died, reciting them in his head as if he was making a quick roll call, remembering how Eilidh had told him of them of all in a letter he received one day.

Murdo Mackay, Skigersta, aged 19, killed in France... John Gunn, Knockaird, age 21, killed in France... Alex Smith, Fivepenny, aged 22, killed in France... Donald

Smith, Habost, killed in France, aged 20... Angus Campbell, Habost, aged 20...

And then there were the ones whose faces he could recall, those who lived close to his home.

John Macdonald, 16 North Dell, killed by gas poisoning, aged 22... Murdo Murray, 5 South Dell, killed in Flanders, aged 31... Donald Graham, 18 South Dell, killed in action in France, aged 20... Donald Morrison, 4 South Dell, killed of gas poisoning in Flanders, aged 20...

It was those who had been poisoned by gas that he found hardest to picture, their tearing at the top buttons of their tunics as it burned their throats, their lungs turning to liquid as they spluttered, gasping for breath. That wasn't to say that there hadn't been moments at sea when he hadn't felt much the same way. One slip and into the depths. Water clouding lungs. Salt crusting skin like the mud that cloaked those in the trenches. Seabirds swooping down and tearing flesh. Fish, crabs and sharks waiting to feast upon you. There were days even when the ocean was steady and calm that life had fallen from men's fingers. An accident. A moment of carelessness. He recalled Foster diving into the sea near Harwich when he realised that someone had fallen from the deck of the *Glengarry*. He didn't reach him; the young man's body sucked within the whirl and whoosh of the propellors. Tormod recalled looking down at the sea after this occurred, seeing the red tinge of the churning water, and turning aside to vomit, a long trail of sickness spilling from his throat.

His gorge rose at other times too, when he discovered some of his neighbours – Donald Morrison in the above list, Norman Morrison, John Murray, Alex Macdonald, Kenny Graham – had been gassed, shot or bayoneted in areas that were alien to them, from the Dardanelles to Vimy Ridge, the Aegean Sea to the Somme. These were men who wanted no more than the narrow limits of their old world – Dùn Àrnaistean, Buaile Na Crois, Na Cnipean Àrd, Loch Dìobadal, Beinn Dail, Àirigh na Glaice, Loch Mharabhat – yet news of their passing far from these places had come in short and hurried notes, written in English, a language that had never really passed their lips until they departed their own shoreline. The landscape where they had walked and wandered was now haunted by their absence. He wondered if the villages they came from would ever get over their leaving, the manner of their passing so random and cruel.

It was different now. It lightened his spirits that telegrams were being sent for different reasons. No longer just missives notifying people of death, but telling instead of transport arrangements, ways of going home, the men trying their best to make their language as brief and condensed as possible.

```
Arriving early tomorrow STOP In Barvas
meet with horse STOP

Sailing soon for Stornoway STOP See you
tomorrow STOP

Now in Kyle STOP Village men home
tomorrow morning STOP
```

```
Kill sheep STOP Home tomorrow STOP

Both Iolaire and Sheila sailing STOP
Hoping to sail on the first faster ship
STOP See you tomorrow STOP

Will make way to Ness on boat after
Stornoway arrival STOP Not long now STOP

Leaving soon on Iolaire STOP See you soon
STOP
```

They chuckled as they read their messages aloud, declaring, too, how little they had spent on the telegrams; the girl laughing as she noted each word down.

'I've heard you islesmen were mean but I didn't know the half of it,' she giggled. And then a few moments later, she confessed, 'We haven't had a day like this since the day we were told the war had ended. Not the half of it.'

'What happened then?' someone asked.

'We hung out all our sheets, towels and pillowcases from the windows. It looked like a proper washing day. The banging of kettles and pots. Rattles of spoons. Noise the likes of which this place had never heard before.'

'Someone's doing the same just now over in Skye,' one of the sailors pointed out.

'Oh…?'

They looked over the water towards Kyleakin. A white sheet was flapping on top of Caisteal Maol, the stone ruin on the edge of the village. It could barely be seen in the mist that shrouded the island, a jagged tooth on the other side of the narrow channel of water. The sheet's beat and fervour contrasted with the stillness of Kyle. All that seemed to move there were gulls. Squawking and flapping, they terrified Roddy Murray each time they came near. He'd raise his arms to his face to protect himself from them, shaking terribly.

'Brutes,' he mumbled. 'I saw what they did to the men who landed in the sea after the Battle of the Falklands. Both the dead and the living. Damn albatrosses. Damn birds. As if there weren't enough dead fish in the water for them to feed upon, floating all around. And then a few weeks later, some of the bodies would wash up on the shoreline. Eyes pecked out. Bones scraped clean.'

It didn't take long for Tormod to discover all there was to see in Kyle: the Station Hotel; the post office where all the mail for the islands had been gathered for the boat, the *Sheila*, waiting at the pier; the Chemist's Corner; Railway Terrace; the Church of Scotland with its strange window that looked like a glass flower above the pulpit. Unlike some others, he wasn't interested in the train that was at a halt there – with its cargo of mines – bound for Invergordon a short time later. He had seen Charlie and some of the other libertymen in their uniforms on their knees beside it, examining how it blew and billowed steam, its wheels, chimney, the pistons that drove it onwards, how it was hitched together, how its links and bolts were formed with weight and complexity. He saw how one of the men touched it shyly with his hands, coming away from that contact with soot and stains on his fingers and palms, blacker by far than anything Tormod had ever brushed against in his smithy.

'Now that's a proper welcome,' one of the Skyemen waiting there muttered, looking across the sea to his native island, the white sheet that was flapping there. 'Not like the cold one we're getting in Kyle.'

'Hoy…' the girl said, laughing once again. 'We're doing our best for you. A lot better than any Skyeman truly deserves.'

And there were other reasons for laughter. John Campbell, from the village of Cross, who came up to Tormod and showed him the silk scarf and shawl he had bought for his wife in Gibraltar. 'Not sure if they were a terribly good idea. I can't see her wearing them to either the kirk or the peat-stack.' The man from Leurbost in Lochs who told him that the last time he had been home on leave, his daughter Catherine had run away from home at the first sign of his approach, thinking her grandfather was her father and this man was a stranger who had come to her mother's bed. 'I hope to stay around longer this time,' he said to Tormod, 'win her to my ways.' The fellow, too, that informed him the reason he had gone to war was that the minister had said people were breaking the Eighth Commandment and it was his duty to put an end to it. '*Thou shalt not steal.* Well, from what I noticed, a lot more stealing went on after the war started than ever went on before.'

Yet, of all these encounters, it was the one Tormod had in the Red Cross tent with Angus Thomson that he most remembered – the young man sidling up to him in his seat, his crop of curly red hair, eyes bowed and avoiding his gaze. He sat there for a long time before he turned their grey shade in Tormod's direction, a smattering of freckles on his unlined face.

'You know who I am?' he asked.

'No.'

'Oh… I thought your Eilidh might have mentioned me,' he said, blushing, freckles blending with the bright shade of red.

'No. She didn't.'

'Oh…'

'Why should she have mentioned you?' Tormod asked.

'Oh, I'm Angus Thomson. I met your sister in the kirk a few years ago. Before the war started. It was just a few words in the beginning. We met again in the kirk last summer when I was home on furlough. We decided we would get married when all this was over. I've got a house in Borve. Well, it's my parents' home but…'

His voice trailed away, disappearing into the rumble of other voices in the tent. It became as slight as his narrow shoulders, the wisp-like shape of the man.

'Sorry. I don't know anything about this.'

'I thought she'd have told you. But I suppose she's got so much on her mind at the moment. What with your mum and dad being ill. She must barely have a moment…'

Tormod stopped, conscious that this stranger knew more about his own family than he did.

'They're ill?'

'Your father has taken to his bed. Still snapping orders in everyone's direction. Your mother's a frail shadow of herself.'

'I wouldn't worry about my father. As soon as I get home, he'll get well. It'll give him an excuse for shouting out more instructions. He'll be like that till the day the Devil comes to take him.'

Angus laughed. 'Eilidh says he's stubborn.'

'Aye. He is that. But why didn't she tell me he was ailing?'

'It would only have troubled you,' the young man smiled. 'She's lucky that Catriona's around to help her. She'd be lost without her.'

'Aye.' For the first time in ages, he thought about his wife. Her small breasts, thin legs, bony ribcage and shoulders came into his mind, her skin shimmering as if she had the shape and substance of a ghost. He shivered, shaking himself into a recollection of her good qualities, her fidelity to him, her faith in God, how she never criticised him in front of others, the way she never stopped working through her days. She was so unlike his first wife, Morag. A more solid, substantial figure, she used to divert him from his work much of the time, coaxing him down to the shoreline when he was working in a field, taking his hand and guiding him to the shadow of a haystack. He loved the loudness of her laughter – a sound that he could never imagine from Catriona's lips. Nevertheless, he had learned to appreciate her over the last few years. She had her virtues too. 'She's a good, hard-working woman,' he said.

'Aye.'

Tormod shook his head, choosing to alter the direction of the conversation. 'So what did you do in the war?' he asked.

'I was in the RNR like most of the ones here. I was in the Dardanelles.'

'What was that like?'

'I'm not sure how much I remember about it,' he began before he started speaking of the boat leaving Moudros Bay in Lesbos with 'thick fog upon the water' and heading in the direction of the Dardanelles, 'delivering supplies to the men who were fighting the Turks up in Kumkale, crates filled with bully beef, dried fish for the soldiers to chew and swallow in their trenches'. It wasn't long after they landed that 'the firing started. I threw myself down on the deck, trying to avoid the bullets that were winging their way past me. I wasn't successful. A bullet hit me in the calf of my right leg. All I remember for the next while was a fog of French, English and Greek voices, even a Gaelic word or two. That and the pain. The pain was unbelievable. Someone lifted me. Someone brought me to shore.'

Young Angus was shaking as these words flooded from his mouth. Unable to stem or halt their flow, he looked momentarily as if he would be unable to bear the weight of all that had happened to him during the years of conflict. He glanced across at Tormod for a moment before he looked away again, dodging all contact with his eyes.

'There was another time, too, when I was on a boat that went down. In the Med. When I was in the water, I grabbed a hold on this wooden board and clutched onto it, swimming through the darkness. There were all these other voices around, shouting out for me to come and save them. I ignored them. I shut my ears to them all. I knew that the piece of wood I was clinging on to would hold only one, so I pretended not to hear them, turned my head away, even though I knew they were drowning. Tell me… was I wrong in doing that? I was wrong, wasn't I?'

'No. You weren't wrong.' Tormod shook his head. 'Most men here would have done the same.'

'That doesn't make it right…'

'No. But it makes it understandable and easy to forgive.'

Angus tore at his fingers, glancing away again. 'Sorry… Sorry. I didn't mean to blab all that out.'

'It doesn't matter.'

'It's just that I know I've got to talk about all these things before I go home. The likes of Eilidh won't understand about it. Will she? She won't have a clue what the whole thing was like. I know I can never let her know scared I was, how frightened.'

'It's all right…'

'Well, I was petrified. Shitting myself most of the time. Permanent diarrhoea.'

'Angus…'

It was at that moment than one of the few Lowlanders among the men, a tall, thin individual called Jamieson, came into the tent. He was laughing loudly to himself, speaking loudly to everyone that was gathered there.

'You'll never guess what that damn fool Mason did when he brought the *Iolaire* in just now? He banged it hard against the pier. Made a big dent in its bow.' He giggled once again. 'You wouldn't believe it! What an idiot! It's not a good sign! It's not a bloody good sign!'

1936

'According to legend, people learned to see here for the first time.'

My grandad was standing on the crest of Buaile na Crois, a ridge that was near the beginning of our croft. A field of green oats nearby thrashed about in the wind below us, their seeds like tiny bullets clinging to each stalk. On the other side of the hill, we had made our way past a crop of potatoes, white flowers blossoming like a sprinkling of snow. On his shoulder, there was a canvas haversack – not unlike the one I had noticed Shonnie the postman carrying as he made his way through the village on his bicycle, lashed by wind and rain.

'Do you know why?' he turned and asked me.

'No.'

'It was where they first caught a glimpse of the temple in Eoropie. The one they called St Moluag's. They used to go there from all across the island looking for cures and remedies for the diseases they were suffering. People made this little cairn of rocks to celebrate the chance of a miracle. Some say there was even a little wooden cross here once. Every time I go near it, if I have time, I try to remember to place a pebble on its top. Just to remind me what happened there. The good God can do in the world of men. Sometimes we all need reminding of that.' He turned to me. 'Can you see it out there? It's a little grey building not far from the sands.'

I strained my eyes to catch a glimpse of it. At the far end of the headland at the northern tip of the island where the red sandstone lighthouse stood, it looked small and inconspicuous, the waters churning a short distance away from its walls, the bright yellow of the sand. I imagined it would have looked much more noticeable all those centuries before, when the houses that surrounded it would have been huddles of stone, burrowed deep in the ground. 'I think I can.'

'Good.' He handed his haversack to me. 'I want you to have that.'

'Thanks.' My hands stretched out for it. 'What is it?'

'Open it. It's my way of teaching you to see for the first time.'

I fumbled with excitement as I unbuckled it. Inside there was a clutch of pencils and a red, linen-covered journal, not unlike the one he possessed himself, for all it had a different shade.

'Grandad,' I gasped. 'Thanks. Thanks. Thanks.'

He held out his hand once again, raising his palm. 'Don't thank me. I want to teach you how to draw. The way one of the men who was at sea with me taught me. You willing to learn?'

'Of course…'

'Then give me a pencil.'

He sat down on one of the larger stones at the top of Buaile na Crois and began to sketch, using that pencil to gauge the size and scale of the lighthouse, the round, white foghorn by its side. He did this carefully, later brushing the paper lightly with its lead tip to show light and shade. 'Don't ever press too hard,' he said. 'Light and easy. Otherwise, you'll only break the tip.' He nodded in my direction one time he went wrong. 'There's a rubber in the haversack. Get it out...'

And all the time he was talking, telling me about the lighthouse, how its beam flashed white every five seconds, different from every other lighthouse on the coast.

'I memorised that just before I went to war. Just in case I ever sailed past it in the dark of night and I didn't know I was near home.'

And then there were stories of some of the other places at the edge of the village I might one day draw, old myths and legends – though I was conscious, sometimes, that he was making things up, weaving tales out of his own imagination as he set these sketches down on the paper before him. There was Loch Dìobadal where, a short distance from the shoreline, a water-horse or *each-uisge* was supposed to emerge from time to time, setting out to carry a young man or woman on its back, plunging them into its depths. There was Sgeir Dhail, a rocky outcrop that lay a short distance from the coastline of the village. I had heard seals sometimes call out from it, the grey sheen of their bodies contrasting with the dark of the rock on which they sat, the froth and foam that often washed over it.

'A long time ago, out there in that part of the village we call Aird,' he said, indicating where it was with a nod of his head, 'there lived a man and his wife. They weren't the happiest of couples. Sometimes the man would shout and swear at the woman for hours on end. Sometimes he would hit her with his fists. Now, the main reason for their quarrels was the fact that they didn't have a family. "You've let me down!" the man would yell. "I wanted children to help me work this croft, look after me in my old age, and you've given me none! I should never have married the likes of you." And there were times when his anger was so great that he'd be cruel to all of God's creatures, hurting and tormenting their dog, neglecting their sheep, even killing the baby seals he found down on the sands at Tràigh Dhail with a rock.'

I shuddered as I heard this, but his story washed on.

'As time went by, the woman grew more and more sick of all his cruelty and she made up a plan to bring it to an end. One night, when the moon and sea was still and quiet, she took a white shawl she had knitted and brought it out on a boat to Sgeir Dhail. She draped it on a rock there so her husband could see it in the morning.

'The next day, she told him that she had been troubled all night by a dream. She had heard a child crying out on Sgeir Dhail, a human baby left on the rocks by seals who had saved him when his mother tried to drown him in the waves. He laughed at this, telling her she was talking nonsense, but a short time later, he looked out in the direction of the Sgeir. When he saw the shawl lying there, he decided that her story might be true.

'That night and the night after that too, she complained once again of the crying she had heard. "There's a child out there," she told him, "one that is meant for me and you." The moment came when he could take no more of it. Though it was cold and stormy, he went out in his boat, rowing in the direction of Sgeir Dhail, desperate to take home the child he believed to be lying on the rock.

'There were only the seals to meet him. They were all sheltering from the waves that the wind had whipped up, clinging to the coldness of the Sgeir. He reached down his hand to lift the shawl that was lying there, believing a human child was underneath it. To his horror, he discovered a young seal. Its teeth clamped round his fingers. One by one, the other seals turned on him too.

'They must have known what kind of man he was, what cruelties he had done not only to their kind, but also to the woman with whom he shared his life. And they took their revenge on him. He never stepped on board that boat to return home.'

There were other places he mentioned too. Asmigarry, that green space on the moor with a stone house at its centre. The river at the northern end of the village, near the spot where they had distilled whisky long ago. The mill with its water-wheel. Dùn Àrnaistean with its now vanished broch that once stood on the foreland near the shore. People had gone for shelter there when there was trouble on the seas, boats approaching in attack. He said that there were fairies, too, who lived there now that the people who first used it were gone. They sometimes visited the wells that were within the village boundary, turning the minister's well dry.

'There's a little cave there,' he said, grinning. 'A wonderful place to draw.'

'They might have gone for shelter there too.'

'Perhaps. Though they'd have to watch in case the tide came in.'

And then the wind turned chill. He buttoned up his jacket. 'We've been sitting too long here,' he said, and gestured towards the journal. 'Remember I want to see you drawing, though. Take a chance I never had.'

I nodded, grateful for what he had given me.

'It's a way of looking at the world. Much better than never paying a whit of attention to what's going on.'

As we made our way down the hill, I saw Rachel and Great-Uncle Calum walking round our home, boiled potatoes and grain mashed together in a pan to feed the chickens clustering around their feet. Calum was scarcely moving, his every step an exaggeration of infirmity and weakness, as if the breeze that was beginning to whip up around the house was picking up speed and strength. Rachel was trying her best to help him, holding onto his arm in case he might slip and fall. My grandad laughed loudly at the sight.

'That's some performance,' he said. 'That brother of mine should be in the Empire Theatre in Glasgow. He'd find his proper place there!'

Tormod's Journals

December 1918

Tormod thought about the men who crammed aboard the *Iolaire* for much of the rest of his life. He even drew pictures of their faces in order to keep them in his mind, using the sheet of paper which acted as a marker for the Bible he read each night and morning, turning to the pages, say, of the Book of Psalms – *He stilled the storm to a whisper; the waves of the sea were hushed* – to both open and close the day. It was something that Catriona disapproved of, sniffing each time he took the thin slip out. 'It's akin to blasphemy,' she said to him one evening. 'All this pondering on the dead.'

Tormod shook his head. 'It's better than forgetting them.'

'I'm not sure,' she said. 'There's been so many. We can get lost in our thoughts of them.'

'Aye. That's true enough. But it's also one good reason to try and keep them all in mind.'

He sketched pictures of both his fellow islanders and the officers who had been responsible for the way they had all squashed together in the lounge and on deck that evening. And he imagined the conversations that took place on board – among themselves and with the nearby crew of the mailboat, the *Sheila*, which was tied up alongside. Tousle-haired men in their Navy uniforms. Others who were thin and gaunt with their heads shaved. One who sported a thick dark moustache.

Among them was the *Iolaire*'s captain, Richard Mason, a broad-shouldered, bulky man in his mid-forties. Over the years, I have imagined and read enough about him to form my own portrait of his personality and character, working out – to the limits of my own satisfaction – exactly how he thought. He would have liked to have been anywhere other than Kyle of Lochalsh that evening. He would certainly have preferred to be either at his family home outside Sheffield or somewhere across the Minch when the bells rang in the New Year later that night – in the arms, perhaps, of his wife, Lucy, some eighteen years younger than him. He longed to hear the tinkle of her laughter chime through midnight, listen to the peal of her voice, too, when he woke up by her side the following morning.

But this was not to be. Instead, he was standing on the bridge of the *Iolaire,* listening to Lieutenant Commander Walsh, who was in charge of proceedings in the port of Kyle. The older man was pleading with him to take as many passengers as possible on board for the voyage. He reported that Captain Cameron on the *Sheila* had told him he could not yet say the number he could accept on board his vessel. ('I have others to think about,' Cameron had declared, shrugging his shoulders. 'Those who sail back and forth all the time.')

'Besides, the *Sheila* already took twenty-two stranded in Kyle on Monday night,' Walsh confessed. 'I feel I have imposed on Captain Cameron enough.'

Mason listened long and hard to Commander Walsh's argument. Aware that he had only taken charge of this vessel when it arrived in Stornoway just before Armistice Day, he kept looking in the direction of his Chief Officer, Lieutenant Cotter, to see if he had any answers to the Commander's questions. His fellow crewman only dipped his eyes and looked the other way.

'Besides, I don't know how I'm going to face these Lewismen if I tell them they're going to have stay another night here. We might have a riot on our hands.'

'I can appreciate that,' Mason said. 'And God knows over the last years they've had a lot of training to undertake a proper one.'

A smile flickered, only to be doused a moment later by a frown. 'If push came to shove, could you take three hundred men?'

'Yes. We could take that easily enough.'

Cotter looked doubtfully at him. 'We've only boats for one hundred people. Eighty life jackets or so… We're short-handed too. It'll be more than a tight squeeze.'

Mason grinned, his smile revealing much of the contempt that military men have for civilian regulations. 'We should be all right. At least we've got one thing going for us. It's a calm night. And it'll be a lot calmer for the people of Kyle when these men are on their way.'

He probably had doubts about that a short time afterwards when he saw how many were piling out of the railway carriages during the late afternoon and evening. His legs began to buckle. It was as if the entire port was about to be submerged in a great dark tide. More and more black uniforms seemed to be appearing out of nowhere. More and more strong-armed men anxious to get home to their crofts and fishermen's houses, their daughters, sons and wives. It was as if he were among the audience at the Sheffield Empire, watching some great conjuring trick being performed before his disbelieving eyes, a long black handkerchief being pulled out of a top hat, a tribe stepping out of an empty wardrobe on stage.

'There are far too many of the beggars,' he muttered.

But he suppressed these thoughts as the men came on board, greeting them as they arrived. My grandfather was among them, taking note of those he recognised; some of those he did not. He nodded in the direction of John Finlay Macleod, a man he had last seen in the church when the minister delivered a sermon asking them to sign up.

'Not long to go now,' Tormod said, smiling.

'Aye.' The man from Port grinned shyly. 'I'm looking forward to taking my shoes and socks off and taking a walk in the sands.'

'Perhaps even a dip in the sea.'

'You'll have to take off your uniform for that,' he said. 'It's probably the wrong time of year too.'

'You might be right about that.'

There was Am Patch, too, nodding in his direction as he entered the lounge. Tormod stretched out a hand towards him. He had heard that the Knockaird man had been back and forth from Portland down in Dorset to the island just a short time before for his father's final illness, the funeral that followed.

'Sorry to hear about your troubles,' Tormod said.

He responded with a grip more tenacious than any Tormod had ever known, his hand sweeping up his fingers like a spade.

'Thanks,' he said. 'Very kind. Very kind.'

The Harrisman Macdermid, from the *Glengarry*, was there too. He dodged Tormod's gaze, knowing he was doing something that a few might have considered a little dishonest. He was meant to wait for another vessel rather than board the *Iolaire*, something that might not arrive till Thursday – the second of January. 'There's no point in that,' he muttered to a few others from his native island. 'The Skyemen are going back to Portree on the *Jenny Campbell* in a few hours' time. The Lewismen are sailing on the *Iolaire* or *Sheila*. Why should we always be the ones who are treated second best? Beside, we could easily walk to Tarbert and beyond. What's wrong with that?'

And so some of them had sneaked aboard. Just like the man he met from Lochs, slipping under the railings from the *Sheila* to the other vessel. The *Iolaire* was larger than the mailboat, made – unusually – of iron and not steel. One of his friends had argued that this would make it a lot more brittle under the force and impact of the waves, but he shook his head at this.

'It's fairly calm tonight and the yacht will be a lot faster,' he explained.

The ones who had arrived first had time to appreciate the luxury of their vessel, admiring the panels that were in the lounge, the full-length mirror in the saloon. Even Macdermid had halted for a moment or two before that, using his reflection to tidy up his Navy uniform. Another man jostled behind him, using the glass to mirror back his impersonation of a hen, his back bent, shoulders crouched as he clucked.

'*Buk – buk – buk – buk – bacagh – buk – buk – bacagh – buk – buk – buk – buk – buk – buk – buk – bacagh…*'

A moment or two later, one of the new arrivals was standing before a ship's lamp, making the silhouette of a bird with his finger, one with a hooked beak and dark wings that flapped and fluttered against a wall.

'*Seall! Iolair!*' he laughed, explaining what he said a moment or two later in English. 'Look! The *Iolaire*! An eagle!'

One of the few passengers from the town, Jamieson, talked about how posh and plush it was, delving into the history of the boat – how in peacetime it had once belonged to the Duke of Westminster, how it had been once called the *Amalthea*, being given the title *Iolaire* as this was the name of the base in Stornoway.

'We're very privileged to be on it. Very lucky indeed. All a sign of how well our betters and superiors look after our every need.'

A few minutes later and they discovered just how fortunate they really were. They heard Mason shout and yell, Lieutenant Cotter echoing him.

'Right! That's enough. We're already overloaded.'

'The rest of you will have to go on the *Sheila*. There's no room here.'

There was mumbled discontent, an angry yell or two.

'No ifs. No buts… Why don't you lot count your blessings? At least you're getting home soon. Think of the poor Harrismen. They're not getting home for ages.'

Tormod sneaked a glance in the direction of Macdermid, but he said nothing.

'That's it then. That's it.'

After that, there was the clatter of the gangway, the brisk tap of feet running along the deck. Tormod took out a few sheets of paper from his kitbag. There were a few interesting engravings on the wood panels of the boat. The outline of a goat with a young child lying not far from its feet. A sprinkling of stars. A bearded man wrapped in a sheet with lightning sparking from his outstretched hand. He didn't understand any of it, but drawing these figures would pass an hour or two until sleep overcame him or the boat reached Stornoway, reminding him of another way of life, far from the blackhouses and byres of his home village. He shoved them in his pocket as he completed them, folding each one – together with a locket and bracelet – in the little piece of oilcloth he had in his possession. Another man was bringing a small concertina out of his kitbag, unwrapping it from the silk shirt in which it had been stored. 'I'll have no use of that in Shader,' he declared. Just before he was about to start playing it, one of the older men stood up and held out his hand.

'A word of prayer first,' he declared. 'Anything else would be disrespectful to the Lord who chose to deliver us from all these years of conflict.'

He began to speak then, his voice loud and resonant over the thrum of the boat's engine, the waters turning between the vessel's hull as it moved away from the quay.

'Lord,' he said, 'we are all men of the sea here and know – only too well – how, in the words of Psalm 93, *the floods* can be *lifted up, how they* can *lift up their voice; how the floods lift up their waves* and bring men to destruction. We have seen this in the loss of so many of our friends and loved ones. Sometimes even the very ships that we have sailed upon have perished, lost to the depths of the ocean, the heart of the fire, and we have emerged as the survivors, but still doused and stained by that water, still scorched by the flame. Yet we know too that *the Lord on high is mightier than the noise of many waters, yea, than the mighty waves of the sea*, and we commit ourselves to His mercy, as we have done so many times before. Bless the men who sail here with us. Stand guard over them and their families, yet even if Thou choose to take us, in the middle of this night, in the centre of this voyage, remain with us, be patient with our follies for we know that *the Lord reigneth, he is clothed with majesty; the Lord is clothed with strength, wherewith he hath girdled himself...* He will stand by us, both now and through eternity if we choose to give our faith to the Lord...'

1936

'*Thuit e! Thuit e!*'

I don't know what startled us most that day – the fact that Rachel was speaking at all, or the way in which she was yelling in Gaelic, a language we had never heard on her tongue. It made me look up from the drawing I was sketching. It made my grandma do something I'd never heard her do before – respond in English to the little girl who, her face blanched, her dark curls pasted against her cheeks, had rushed into our home.

'Who fell?'

'Great-Uncle Calum.'

'Oh. Where did he fall?'

'Round the back of the house.'

We rushed out to find him on his back there, sprawled out at the foot of some steps that led to the blackhouse roof. The other thing we noticed was the shape of a bone jutting out of the bottom of his trouser leg. His good hand clenched as he tried to deal with the pain. The side of his face that could shift and move was caught in a grimace.

'What on earth happened?' Grandma asked.

'He clumbed up to the thatch to get some eggs that had been left there. I told him not to…' Rachel began.

'But the damn fool didn't listen,' Calum muttered, his

face set in self-mockery. 'Help me up and never mind what happened. I'll be all right in a moment.'

We looked at him lying there in the crushed grass and dandelions, wondering whether or not he had noticed the injury he had caused to himself. Knowing him so well, we couldn't decide whether he was actually aware of what had occurred or if he was just seeking to fool himself about what had just happened.

'Help me up,' he pleaded. 'I'll be back on my feet in no time.'

I moved to obey him but my grandma stretched out a hand to halt me. 'Wait…' she said. 'We have to be sure.'

'Catriona.'

'We don't want to cause you any more damage than we can help,' she said before turning to me again. 'Alasdair. Go and get your grandad. Rachel. See if you can get a few of the neighbours. Tell them we may need an old door or the sail of a boat.'

'Catriona,' he hissed. 'We don't need that. We don't need that.'

'Yes, Calum. We do. We can't move you otherwise without taking a risk.'

He cursed and fulminated after that, calling her a pious bitch and wondering if it was possible to get a different kind of woman out of the village of North Tolsta. 'You're all the same! All the bleeding same!' He made a pinched shape with his one proper hand. 'As tightly clamped as the black covers of the Bible. And about as comforting too.'

We tried not to listen to him. Grandma walked away, trembling as she stood beside the far corner of the house, praying to herself and pretending not to hear a word he said. I was racing down the croft, heading to Grandad in the potato field to tell him all that had just occurred; my sister about to share the miracle of her restored voice elsewhere.

'Great-Uncle Calum fell! We need your help.'

The old man was weeping by the time we returned. 'Not the other leg. Not the other leg.' He turned to his brother when he arrived at his side. 'You know what it was like the day I woke up in Liverpool? I knew no one there. Nobody. All I knew was that I went to bed the night before and felt a little cramp in my thigh, as if I couldn't shift it. The next day I couldn't move. The whole world swirling round and round about me. All these voices talking English. I couldn't move. I couldn't move.'

'Shhh…'

'Don't let that happen to me again. Don't let me lose my chance to walk around.'

'No, we won't,' my grandad said. 'Not if we can help it.'

It was on a stretch of canvas tarpaulin that Dòmhnall Stufain and his sons, Angus and Norman, carried him in that day, one that had been used to cover the top of a haystack, prevent the rain and dampness soaking the grass. Together with my grandad, our neighbours buckled and strained as they took him through the doorway, trying to make sure there was neither upset nor disturbance on the way. When they finally reached there, they slipped him on top of the box-bed, wrapping the blankets around him as they did so. When they laid him down, Dòmhnall Stufain reached to pat him, pretending not to see the shimmer of tears on his cheeks. They sparkled in his wrinkles, the lines scored on his face.

'The doctor will be here soon,' Dòmhnall Stufain told him. 'Or the nurse. They'll all be running to help. You're a Very Important Person.'

'An example to us all.'

He gritted his teeth as they filed out; some stopping to ruffle Rachel's hair or to shake my grandad's hand.

'Call us if you need to,' Ruairidh, another of our neighbours, said. 'I've a wee drop of whisky in the house. Might help numb the pain.'

'Aye. Thanks. If we need it…'

And then we were on our own – in the half-light of the house, looking across at Calum, trying our best to cheer him up yet not finding the right words to do so. I could hear the sound of my great-uncle's breath, his chest heaving and shivering from time to time, as if the accident had let loose a terrible terror within him.

'It'll be a long time since the doctor's last been here,' Calum said.

'Since our mother died.' Tormod nodded. 'Ten years or more ago. 1922.'

'Aye.'

'Before then, it was our father. 1919.'

'That's right.' Calum grimaced as another shaft of pain shuddered through him. 'And before that it was Christina.' He paused for a moment, listening to the tick of the clock, a spark or two in the peat fire. 'I wonder how she's getting on.'

'God knows.'

'Aye. He truly does. Stuck in that hospital with all those lost and lonely people, each as angry and confused as she is. No hope of a cure.' He shook his head. 'Isn't it amazing how neighbours run around to help if a part of the body's broken? Yet if the mind's shattered, no one turns up.'

'Aye.'

'It's the same with Eilidh's husband, Angus Thomson, up in Borve. Never right since the war. Bothered with his nerves. All that trembling and shaking that he suffers. And no one goes to see him. Not even us.'

'Well, they live a piece away,' Grandad said, trying to defend himself.

'A lot nearer than Murdo in Barvas. Yet we go and see him. And he comes to see us.'

'That's easier in other ways.'

'That's what I mean…' Calum began.

My grandad didn't let him finish that sentence. He rose from his seat and placed a couple of peats on the fire. I could see his hand was quaking, a shiver passing through his arms and legs. It looked for a moment as if he was about to stumble, his balance gone after his brother's words.

'There's a good reason why I don't seek out the likes of Angus Thomson. The memory of that night's within me. I don't want anyone or anything to wake it up. It's why I turn away from Iain Help any time he's in the village, why I turn my back, too, on the likes of John Finlay Macleod and Am Patch. It's probably the reason why they also feel better if they turn away from me. It's not that I dislike these men. In fact, anything but. It's because we also have that day in common.'

'And you don't want to think about it?'

'Aye. Exactly that.'

Grandad shook himself, looking down at Rachel and me.

'Come on, you two. Let's go for a walk out towards Loch Dìobadal. We don't want to be here when the doctor or nurse comes.'

'Tormod…'

'No, Calum. It wouldn't be good for the children if they were here. There's a time in life when you're forced to deal with such things. There's a time, too, when you're best off avoiding them.'

It was the strangest walk we ever went on with him that afternoon. Our grandad headed in a different direction from the usual way he took us – past Loch Dìobadal with its lapping waters, a swan or two floating on its surface, pointing with his walking stick towards Aird, the small patches of heather among the green, the stream winding and trickling towards the coast where there was this mound, as smooth and curved – though this was never said during that walk – as a woman's breast. At the same time, he was talking, mentioning how rusted swords had been found below the surface there, discovered by two brothers who lived on the southern edge of the village. 'They're now in the National Museum,' he said. 'Down in Edinburgh.'

His voice began to quicken, matching his step. It wasn't long before Rachel and I were having to run to keep up with him, tripping occasionally as we did so.

'They're from the eighth century. Imagine that. These swords from the eighth century. Even back then young lads, not much older than you, were trying to pin someone of their own age with a sharp tip of iron or bronze or some other kind of metal, seeking to kill one of their fellow islanders for the sake, say, of a sheep or a cow. And nothing's changed since then. Nowadays it's Italians trying to steal a few miles of desert sands from the grip of an Abyssinian, Spaniards squabbling over desert rock, Germans and Russians, lads from Edinburgh and Glasgow joining in on their sides. All fools. All stupidity. All vanity.'

He paused, standing still for a moment as he tried to catch his breath.

'Well, let me tell you what war is. War is all the tales I heard that night when I came home on that dark ship. War is oil and fire and steel, hot and slippery and scorching your fingers. War is finding a rope escaping from your hands, the paint on the side of a lifeboat bubbling and too hot for you to touch. War is hearing other men scream and knowing you can do nothing to help them. War is being cold and shivering. War is being alone. War is the company of other men suffering. War is…'

Aware that he had said too much, he stopped then. His attention seemed to be drawn by the birds that were soaring around him. The pulsing wings of the snipe. The weeping of the curlew. The oystercatchers with their persistent, pleading cries.

'Shhh…' he whispered.

We listened to all that was going on, glad he had stopped speaking at last.

'Shhh. You can hear the lapwings. Always remember you can hear the lapwings.'

Tormod's Journals

December 1918

Dark water skidded by. The only chips in its murky half-light were made by an occasional houselight near the shoreline of Raasay or the north-east coast of Skye, the shimmer of the *Iolaire*'s own lights reflected on the darkness of the waves, sometimes tinged with the red curtains of the lounge, the blue drapes of the saloon. There was the strum of the engine, too, as the bow cut through the miles and fathoms that divided them from their homes. The crofthouses where the women they knew lay dreaming, their nights unsettled by the prospect of their men coming home, the thoughts of their arrival weighted with expectation, both the joys and troubles that their presence might bring.

And all of the time, Tormod could hear the thrum of voices. Men talking among themselves, aware that in some cases, it would be the last time they would ever meet. Even though they might have served together, most came from different, distant parts of the island. There were miles of moor between their houses, stretches of coast between one district and the next, even the deep water of a sea loch. As a result, sudden, surprising secrets were told. Men gobbled out stories, conscious that many of the individuals around them would soon become strangers, people they were unlikely ever to see again when they stepped upon their villages roads once more, walked upon their crofts and shoreline. One man – Tormod never even got his name – began speaking about watching the *Invincible* go down at the Battle of Jutland.

'God. It was meant to be unsinkable, unconquerable. And then there were more than a thousand men all gone in one huge and terrifying flash of heat, one that took the hair, eyebrows and moustache off the face of an officer standing near to me. I remember looking at him and giggling, only stopping myself by thinking how glad I was that I had put my hand to my eyes when the blast happened. A moment or two afterwards and I lowered it to see this huge column of black smoke, one that carried at its edges pieces and fragments of some other ships that were nearby. That cloud seemed to take ages to get to its full height. Up, up in the sky. And then it rained and thundered bits of fallen debris, metals pinging and bouncing on the turret, the top of the shield where I was in position with my 4" Naval gun, the lascars loading shells. Like a damn fool, I burned myself when I picked up one of the pieces that had fallen, the officer with the shorn moustache laughing and calling me a clown for doing that.' He thrust out his hand to prove the truth of his story, the wound still raw and scorched on his skin. 'And all I remember thinking was that the night before, some of the younger officers on the *Invincible* had been on board our ship, eating and drinking and having a good time. I remember how guilty I felt at cursing them when they woke me with their racket. Not that they didn't deserve it with their antics.'

Even John Macdermid from Harris seemed to be affected by this behaviour. He stepped towards Tormod, a little shy and embarrassed. Words prised open his lips.

'I'm sorry the two of us never got on,' he said.

'That's all right. Trouble like that sometimes happens.'

'It's just that I was worried about you. One of our own.'

Tormod said nothing.

'Just that I thought you had been snared by all the transgressions and perversities that can be found in the outside world. *The wicked desireth the net of evil men, but the root of the righteous yieldeth fruit.*'

Again Tormod didn't speak. Looking intently away, he was listening instead to a man at the other end of the saloon singing about the joys of his native island, a location where, according to the words:

> '*Far an robh mi 'n làithean m' òig'*
> *Ruith gun bhròig dol don tràigh,*
> '*S mi ri streap gu nead an eòin*
> *Anns gach còs sam bi àl...*'

> '*Where I was throughout my youth,*
> *running without shoes to the beach,*
> *climbing too to the birds' nests*
> *in each crack and crevice the young can find...*'

And throughout that song, the breeze was picking up, white sea-foam slashing portholes, foam spilling onto the deck, the boat stirring and rocking more than it had been an hour or so before. Their voyage would not be the calm return home they had believed it might be a short time ago. Instead, the wind was likely to escort them into Stornoway, usher them towards the safe shelter of that bay.

'There was something else worrying me too,' Macdermid said, taking out a letter from his inside pocket. It was one he'd creased and uncreased endlessly, wrinkles forming on the page, making many of the words smudged and indecipherable. He passed it towards Tormod, whose gaze scurried over it, unable to read its scrawl. He shrugged to show his lack of interest in it. He had enough troubles of his own.

'My brother keeps going to visit my home. Keeping an eye on my wife and family. Making sure they are well. Or so he says. I think the bleggard has got his beady eye on my land. All these acres he hopes to get his hands on if anything happens to me.'

'Perhaps you're wrong,' Tormod said. 'You have been before about things.'

'Perhaps I'm not. I know what he's like. More full of spite and nastiness than the average Lewisman.'

'Oh, I doubt that,' Tormod said, smiling. 'It would be stretching it for any Harrisman to be as bad as that.'

For an instant, Macdermid puffed out his cheeks, annoyed and agitated at the sarcasm. A moment later, he changed his mind and laughed.

'Perhaps one side is as bad as the other…'

'Perhaps…'

Macdermid sighed. 'Will you join me in a prayer? I'd like to wish you well for the rest of your life.'

'Perhaps,' Tormod repeated, grinning at the same time.

'I'll take it you're not saying no then.'

'No. I'm not.'

The Harrisman clasped his hands together, his words declaring his gratitude at having lived through the war and all its troubles, asking for strength, too, at all that awaited them when they travelled home. 'For our lives there are not free of toil and sorrow. Sometimes we suffer more because of those who are our kin than those who are our foes.'

Tormod nodded, thinking of his brother, father, sister, the daughter Mairi he barely knew, even his wife Catriona waiting for him at home. Each brought their own trials, ushered in their own shadows. That darkness seemed to hover round human existence.

'God, we wonder how long Thou will allow the wicked to be jubilant, for suffering and want to haunt our lives. We ask when the day might come when the arrogant and proud will no longer be victors, when those who fill their days full of idleness will perish and be set aside. Yet we leave these things up to Thee in Thy wisdom and mercy, aware that only Thou hast the answers to these questions, that Thou are aware of the time when these mysteries will be settled and resolved. For all these things, the awareness that Thou are in control, may we be truly grateful. Amen.'

'Amen.'

Tormod nodded his thanks as the Harrisman walked away. He, too, had his own troubles to face when he came back from the war. Not just Catriona. Not just his father. There was one person he had rarely thought of since the beginning of the war, his daughter, Mairi. Aware of the reasons for this, he dodged all thought of her, his absence from her life too raw and painful. It would be a major effort even to reclaim her. During the first week or so he had been at home on furlough, she had even run away from him, curling up beside a calf and hiding in the byre for hours, hoping that the stranger who had come to their home would soon step out the door and disappear. Just like her real mother had done before him. Just like he had done for too long.

He began to sketch her face in his journal, trying to summon her back, but stopping when he realised that he probably would not be able to draw her features accurately or well. He knew how much she had changed since the last time he had seen her. Her face probably no longer possessed the roundness of an infant; cheeks no longer bright and rosy. Her grey eyes would have lost their savage intensity. He stabbed his pencil in frustration, blunting its tip.

'I can't remember. I can't bloody remember.'

He knew that he had felt just like her the day she had hidden from him, shy and frightened, fearing that the rough beast that the war had forced him to become would hurt and damage this child. He stood in awe of her – all her tough fragility, her strange and alien femininity – after all these years in the company of men. He was aware, too, that she saw Catriona, her stepmother, as much more of a parent than he would ever be. She would follow in Catriona's footsteps when she walked to the well for water, unable to stay with him, too, when her grandparents and Calum were absent from the room.

He hoped it would not take too long to win her over. At least he was coming back, not like all those other men of whom he heard the other passengers talk in whispers, their voices becoming hushed each time they mentioned the dead.

'My brother's dead,' one might say. 'Killed off Malta.'

'My own was one of the thousand killed in the *Invincible*. Only six got off that.'

175

'My neighbour was saved from the *Ballycastle*. Taken aboard the *Anthea* and then that was sunk some half hour later. The poor soul had run out of luck.'

They would talk, too, of the vessels they had served on, reciting a litany of names as if they were saying the rosary he had heard Catholics muttering in Ireland and France. Or the catechism they learned in school, full of strange, exotic words – like 'transgression', 'covenant' and 'sanctification' – that stumbled on their lips when they had to repeat them in the classroom. They spoke, too, about the food they had eaten on board.

'There's no doubt it kept us going. A kettle of thick cocoa and a couple of biscuits at quarter past six. Then scrub the decks, forward, aft, water flooding over each inch before we mop it all up and go down to the messdeck for breakfast. Porridge, a kipper if we're lucky. Bread and butter, margarine, sugar now and again. Change into the rig of the day. Clean the ship. Inspection. Gallop round the ship. Leaping hatches. Sliding down ladders. Rifle drill. Seamanship. Signals. Splicing rope. Knots. After that, there's the reward of stewed corned beef…'

'Black and crisp with a few cinders from the funnels,' someone added.

'Aye. And glad to get them. Gave our meal a little bite and flavour.'

'Well, tomorrow we'll be back to the usual. Mutton. Potatoes. Fish.'

'It's all a little better than one of the meals we had on the *Malaya* in the Battle of Jutland,' one of the men mentioned.

'What was that?'

'A shell hit one of the lower decks, shards shattering all over the place. I stepped into the kitchen to find one of the cooks with his head in a soup-pan. It didn't stop the boys eating it. I even took a bowlful of the broth myself. It seemed better than letting it go to waste.'

'Quite right too. Quite right.'

And then in that swirl of words and talk, Tormod heard another man speak about someone he was with in the Battle of Jutland, one of the midshipmen who had been hit.

'He was screaming his head off. "Lost my leg," he kept yelling, "lost my bloody leg. Where the hell did my leg go?" He didn't stop his bawling until someone went off and found it. He took the damn thing in his fingers after that and found some bank-notes he had rolled up and stowed away in his sock. After that, he fell back. Quite content with himself.'

It was as if they were compelled to repeat these kind of tales, frightened that when they arrived home, as John Finlay Macleod said quietly to Tormod, 'they wouldn't be allowed to tell stories like these any more. No one would understand what they were on about or all that they had gone through. War's hard enough to imagine if you've suffered it. The ones that have stayed at home won't have a clue what we're going on about.'

Tormod nodded, seeing that would be the case in his own home. Once, he told John Finlay, he had even received a letter from his sister Eilidh which contained a sentence his brother had asked her to write.

Calum says to remember how lucky you are being away and seeing all these other places. Some of us never had the chance to do that. Some got no farther than Liverpool.

He stiffened with anger as he thought about this, his fingers plucking at the string of his kit-bag.

'How can you tell a man who is half-paralysed that he is wrong? That it is not "lucky" to be "seeing all these other places" at a time when people are killing each other?'

'Aye,' John Finlay agreed, smiling. 'There was a fellow I met in Lionel who said to me that it must be great to be on holiday from here for a wee while. That it meant I didn't have to cut peats or grass for a time.'

'Fool.'

'Aye. A dangerous one. He doesn't even know the level of his own ignorance. There's a lot like that.'

'Including some of the more educated ones.'

The conversation drifted once again. Tormod heard someone talking about the profit that might be made from the fishing now that the conflict was over. 'All that herring around us. All that ling and other fish.' Another was speaking about the money that men could gain from the moorland. 'Not only from burning peat. Though the good people of Stornoway might be persuaded to give us some of the cash that they handed over in the pre-war days for coal from the mainland. But also from sphagnum moss.' He had seen giant bales of the stuff in some of the wharf buildings in Dartmouth, all picked from the brown, sour acres of Dartmoor. It was used as dressing for the troops injured in the Great War. 'Better than cotton wool, it stops bacteria, cleanses wounds. It also stops warts. Skin infections. Contains iodine… Helps healing…'

It did little for madness, Tormod thought as he sat there in the saloon. The force of that seemed to be rife and unbridled, not only in mankind but also within his own family, coming to the surface from time to time as it did in some of God's other creatures. The quiet dog growling and snapping with an unpredictable rage. The cow kicking the woman who fed her within the confines of a byre. The horse – like one in the village he had seen – unable to accept the boundaries it had observed for years before. He could see its fervour in his father's sudden rages, the way his attention veered from one matter to the next. It had been present, too, in his sister, so much so that they had to buckle her in a straitjacket and send her away to Inverness. It was in him too. He had felt its poison with him at various times in his life. When he had lost his wife, he had sunk into its depths, looking at the child he had fathered and barely able to hold onto her, gaze into her face and catch the movement of her eye. It was one reason why Catriona had been suggested to him; those who had done so believing that a new wife might restore a little light and laughter to his existence. Yet Calum had been right to warn him about how easily he had given into the suggestions of others at that time. In his own way, his acceptance of her had been another instance of insanity, one more period in which he had forsaken his reason, cast aside all his doubts and concerns.

It had been the same with the beginning of this journey. He had nurtured a few daft dreams in his head, the thought he could escape his old life, the notion that he could make his living through drawing, travelling to some unknown city elsewhere. All deranged, disturbed, demented. Fancies whirled into existence by some weird delusions that birled around his mind. He shook these thoughts from his head. From now on, he was going to be like most of the people who were on the *Iolaire* with him. All quiet, decent, hard-working men who never gave much consideration to their more frenzied thoughts, forcing them from their heads instead.

It was then the madness really began. He looked up to see Ruairidh Morrison standing in the saloon doorway. His clothes soaked by wave and water, he was shaking his head in bemusement.

'I think they're going into the harbour the wrong way,' he said.

1936

'I looked at the white waves that lashed the reef and boiled against the rocks as if in fury, I felt that there was but a step between us and death. My heart sank within me; but at that moment my thoughts turned to my beloved mother, and I remembered those words, which were among the last that she said to me: "Ralph, my dearest child, always remember, in the hour of danger, to look to your Lord and Saviour Jesus Christ. He alone is both able and willing to save your body and your soul." So I felt much comforted when I thought thereon...'

My words spilled out into the quiet of the room. Outside the snow was falling, flake after flake, drop following drop, turning the entire island white. It had already altered Beinn Dail a few miles away on the moorland into looking as if it had slipped away from its usual landscape and been transformed into Mont Blanc or some other mountain in the Swiss Alps. Every ditch was now covered and concealed, as if much of the island was flat and level without any of the ridges and mounds that were usually seen. Buaile na Crois, the 'view of the cross', upon our croftland looked white and pristine, as if the purity that pilgrims sought generations ago when they kneeled and prayed there, looking out for the chapel in

Eoropie, had been restored once again to it, bringing back the aura of holiness it once possessed.

Our grandma thought that too, nodding as I read aloud to Calum in his bed, his broken leg fixed within a wooden cast. She was impressed by Ballantyne's *The Coral Island*, one of the books I had obtained from Mr MacAskill, the headteacher, when I went to ask him for some I could read to my great-uncle till he recovered and was able to walk once again.

'That's an excellent idea,' he'd declared, taking a few from the shelves and handing them to me. 'It'll do wonders for your reading too. Bring you on in leaps and bounds.'

Clearly it was helping others too. My grandma even mentioned it in her prayers one evening. 'Thank you, Lord, for bringing such a wonderful book to our home. It is good to know that there are learned men of faith who can write books like that. They will bring many to You through the gift of story.' Calum grunted in response to her words. He wasn't so sure about that, preferring Stevenson's *Treasure Island* to Ballantyne's work.

'Och, there's no one quite like Long John Silver,' he argued. 'He brings more delight to me than anyone else.'

'That's only because he's got one leg, like yourself,' Grandad laughed. 'That's what makes you think he's so great.'

'At least I don't have a parrot sitting on my shoulder. Not that there's many of them around here.'

'There's plenty of seagulls,' Rachel added.

We all laughed with a little more gusto than necessary. It was good to hear her speak once again, her voice restored over the past month or so. It made every word she said a miracle, every sound that came from her lips a minor marvel.

'Very good,' Grandad said.

She was sitting on his lap as she often did when they were in the house together. He was teaching her how to tie knots similar to those he had learned as a sailor, his fingers as adept as they had been when forming animal shadows on the wall. The cat lay in front of them, cleaving to the ashes of the fire for warmth.

'The figure eight,' Grandad said, showing her how to do this.

'The bow knot.'

'The cat's paw.'

'Gripping sailor's hitch.'

I began to read again, trying to keep my voice as soft as snowfall, as hushed as the world outside these walls. Calum grinned as I did this, urging me to continue with the tale.

'The ship was now very near the rocks. The men were ready with the boat, and the captain beside them giving orders, when a tremendous wave came towards us. We three ran towards the bow to lay hold of our oar, and had barely reached it when the wave fell on the deck with a crash like thunder. At the same moment the ship struck; the foremast broke off close to the deck and went over the side, carrying the boat and men along with it. Our oar got entangled with the wreck, and Jack seized an axe to cut it free; but owing to the motion of the ship, he missed the cordage and struck the axe deep into the oar. Another wave, however, washed it clear of the wreck. We all seized hold of it, and the next instant we

were struggling in the wild sea. The last thing I saw was
the boat whirling in the surf, and all the sailors tossed
into the foaming waves. Then I became insensible...'

Suddenly Grandad stood up, throwing the rope aside and lifting Rachel from his knee.

'I wish there was something other than shipwrecks in these books.'

I looked over at him. His hands were trembling with agitation; his eyes glowering. Rachel looked startled as she gazed up in his direction, never having seen him act like this before.

'What do you mean?' Calum asked.

'Well, *Treasure Island*, *Kidnapped* and that one... They've all got boats going down in them. Haven't they?'

'I suppose... It makes for a good story.'

'Aye. Well, some of us have lived through them. Some of us know exactly what they're like.'

Nobody said anything to that; the words tumbling into silence like peat crumbling before the heat of a flame. I watched my grandma's gaze darting towards Calum, her eyes startled and afraid.

'You've never talked about that before,' she said.

'No.'

'Some other men have talked about it. But not you.'

He shook his head.

'Not even when the public inquiry was held. You never went there. Refused.'

'Aye.'

'Why now?'

Grandad couldn't answer. Perhaps it was the weather, the way the wind sliced through him these last few days, reminding him of all that had happened that winter's night the *Iolaire* steamed into Stornoway harbour. Perhaps it was the turbulence of the sea as it lashed Sgeir Dhail, the churning of spume in the shadow of the Butt of Lewis lighthouse and its cliffs. Perhaps, too, it was the thought of the death of our mother, his daughter Mairi, that child he had barely known, taken away from him long before her time – not only by her passing, but by the war or, maybe, the time after that, the long shadow that had fallen on the island that New Year's Day, never lifting or fading, being passed down in the seed of the men who had been there from one generation to the next, a sense of gloom, a shadow.

Her death was a reality now that we were present in his house rather than in Glasgow. He could no longer pretend that she might come back one day to see him, wrap her up in that fierce love many men feel for their daughters. He was only aware thoughts of the *Iolaire* were tumbling through his head once again, running amok for all that he had stopped them haunting and troubling him for years. He could see the faces of those who had been with him on that voyage, their expressions still eager and enthusiastic as they talked about all that might come with the peace, their words echoing once more. He could even glimpse their ghosts in each crestfallen wave that rolled onto the shingle-strewn beach below Dùn Àrnaistean, unable even to find shelter there from his memories any more.

'I've no idea. I noticed it first when I was out near Loch Dìobadal the other day, walking with the children. I kept thinking of the war, hoping that no one else would ever have to go through one.'

He avoided looking at his wife and brother, aware what they might be thinking, that the madness that had visited his father and sister was approaching their home once again. Clenching his fists, he hoped that he would have enough force and strength in his mind to resist its coming.

'You will be all right,' Catriona said. 'The Lord will make sure of that.'

Just as she spoke, the door opened. Shonnie, the postman, stepped in. His face was hot and flushed, as if each blast of that blizzard was wearing away a layer of skin. A thin covering of snow sat on his shoulder like a wintry epaulette. There was a little, too, on the brim of his postman's bonnet, like a tiny, intricate fringe of lace.

'Some day,' he said. 'Some day.'

'Aye.' Grandad did his best to smile. 'It certainly is.'

'You must have just been out in it. You're still trembling.'

'Aye. It's bitter. Bitter. On a day like this, people need one another's shelter to survive.' He reached out a hand towards the postman. 'You fancy a cup of tea? It'll put a little warmth in your stomach.'

'No… No. It's best to get a fast pair of boots on today. The sooner I get home to a good blaze the better,' he declared as he placed the letter in my grandad's hand.

A moment later and Shonnie was outside again, blown and buffeted as he stumbled towards a neighbour's house. I watched him from the window, his body set at almost as much of a slant as the snow that was falling, covering the ground. I barely noticed how long Grandad was taking to look at the envelope. Knowing who it was from, he hesitated before opening it, taking a knife to unseal it, cut after cut. He sighed as he took it out.

'It's from your dad,' he declared.

'Is there any money in it?' Grandma asked.

He shook the envelope just to make sure. 'No.'

Grandma clucked her disapproval as he unfolded the sheet. 'She should never have married him. They shared neither faith nor language. A door needs a hinge to allow people to walk together through. They didn't have one. No connection or link.'

He raised up a hand to silence her, his fingers trembling as he read the letter through.

'Oh no,' he said. 'It looks as if I'm going to travel to Stornoway again.'

'What's in it?' I asked.

His voice shaking, he slowly began to read it aloud.

'My dear children. I'm sorry to have taken so long to write, but I have news for you. I have finally found a new job in Aberdeen. It's taken a while but I'll be working at the docks there. This means we can all move home and start our lives together once again. It'll be much easier for me there. I'll have family to help and support me. I also know the place much better than I know Glasgow. I can take you down to the beach there where you can eat all sorts of nice things like ice cream and candy floss, show you both the Don and the Dee. Also to Hazlehead Park where I hear there's a new maze I've never seen before. Pittodrie, too, where we

*can wear a gold and black scarf and cheer on the great
Willie Mills and Matt Armstrong as they score goals
against the Rangers and Celtic. There will be a lot of fun
living in the city. A lot of places we can go.*

*'Words cannot tell how grateful I am for all the help
we have got from Grandma and Grandad over the last
months, a time I have been knocked by grief and sorrow
at the loss of my dear wife…'*

'As if he was the only one,' Calum muttered. 'We all felt
that. We spent a lot more years with her than he ever did.'

'Sssh…' Grandad carried on reading from the letter,
ignoring his interruption.

*'That is all changing now. I will be going up to
Aberdeen next week to start work. After I find a place
to stay, I will write to you and let you all know what
has happened and when you have to travel to Kyle of
Lochalsh for me to come and get you. It's a lot easier
than Mallaig from Aberdeen. Our lives will be a lot
easier too. I know you must be looking forward to
seeing people like your grandmother, aunts and uncles,
your first cousins. You will have a lot of fun there.'*

Grandad paused for a moment. *'With love and kisses,
Dad.'*

Grandad clenched the letter in his hand, the lines on his
forehead knotting. His gaze shifted towards me and then
Rachel a few moments later. His eyes were sparkling with
tears.

'Well…' Great-Uncle Calum said.

Grandma shook her head. 'And, of course, there's no word of money to pay for all of this. No doubt we'll even have to pay for the steamer to take the children to Kyle.'

'There's no chance of that happening,' Grandad declared.

'Aye... No chance.' A voice – harsh and bitter – came from the direction of the bed.

'I took my wee girl to Stornoway harbour. Long time before I thought she was ready for it. I don't want to take the two of them.' Grandad sighed.

It was one of the few times he ever mentioned our mother in our presence. Once, when I asked him why she had left home so young, he had said that she had obtained a job in service down in Glasgow, working for a family in the city's west end. ('She met your dad there not long afterwards. They decided to get married a month or two later.' He shook his head. 'People need others to whom they can belong. Especially when they're in a new place. It's a hand that they can hold onto till they find their own way in their new lives.')

'Perhaps we don't have to send the children back,' Calum said. 'Perhaps we can keep them here.'

'Oh, no... We can't do that. No matter what he's like.' Grandad shook his head. 'Not fair on any man.' He looked across at our grandma, as if he suddenly remembered that she had surrendered a son to her in-laws in North Tolsta on the other side of the island, rarely seeing him ever again. 'Not fair on any human being.'

Grandma smiled thinly, nodding in his direction.

'But it wouldn't be fair to send them away either. Not at this time of year. We wouldn't want them to be stuck in Garve or Achnasheen for hours or days on end. Or even halfway across the moor.' He winked, tilting his head in the direction of the door. 'Aye. We'll use the snow as an excuse for a while. And there's no doubt there's more than a little truth in that tale too. He'll be able to see it for himself if he reads the weather forecast.' He paused again, turning to me. 'You agree on that?'

'Aye.'

'We have a deal. And you, Rachel?'

Her name was spoken into silence.

'Rachel?'

It was then we noticed she was gone…

* * *

She slid out sometime during the conversation, perhaps at the time our grandad had been reading the letter aloud. Stepping into the byre, she slipped on the coat and wellingtons hanging on a hook there and headed into the snow, squeezing open the door silently, going past the smithy and down the croft, making slow progress through fields that almost blended with the white crests of the sea on the horizon, the two merging into each other, surf and snow almost becoming one and the same. It was easy to spot her, the dark pattern of her soles almost the only marks on the surface of the croft, her coat black among all that whiteness, the only life or movement that stood out apart from the swoosh of the wings of an occasional gull or crow. She made her way down the track through the centre of the fields, occasionally stepping across into the spaces where, a short time before, potatoes and turnips had grown, where there was now, perhaps, the crisp stubble of a long-since harvested crop of oats, stiff with frost. Her feet dug into the deep layers of snowfall, firm and steady, testing out the ground that lay before her as she made her way towards the slope of Buaile na Crois with its huddle of stones, its place where pilgrims knelt and prayed.

She even attracted one of the neighbours' attention. From a few doors away, Jessie shuffled in the direction of our house, distracted for a moment from her usual examination of the postcards her sons had sent over the years. 'I noticed her heading out. Where she going in this weather?'

'Not far… Not far.' Grandad turned to me. 'Let's follow her. Just to make sure she's safe.'

We did this, staying a short distance behind, the chill stalling and stiffening our own movements, as if each shift of leg and limb was fixed and dictated by the cold grip of frost and snow. I watched my grandad's breath as he walked alongside me, steam coming from lips and nose, as if he were one of these engines he had last seen in Kyle of Lochalsh, rumbling down the railtrack as if no force on earth could stop and impede us. I could see Rachel before us. Scurrying and slipping among that emptiness as her feet stumbled and fell, she would pick herself up, making her way shorewards, towards the beach that was often treacherous to walk upon even on days when snow was absent, with its layers of shingle and seaween and the river that marked the end of the village, one that flooded sometimes when the tide rolled in. She crossed there, the thickness of the ice holding her, no longer skipping from stone to stone as she usually did when the river rolled free and clear.

'Dùn Àrnaistean. That's where she's heading to.'

Just like he had spoken about it so often to me, he told her of its existence a few days before. The old fort where the people of the district had once gone for shelter when danger threatened and they no longer felt safe and secure in the world. The direction where Shonnie's horse, Flamenco, had raced as it rampaged around the district. Where Grandad's sister, Christina, had run the day she threatened to throw herself off the cliffs. I heard his breath tremble, watched his stride lengthen and speed up.

We padded in that direction, trying to be careful, making sure the ice was firm and strong enough to hold our weight. Even if it cracked, we were aware that it wasn't that deep, that it would do little more than soak our feet and ankles if it gave way.

'Gentle as she goes…'

We found Rachel not far from the Dùn, shivering beside the stone wall that had been built there, her black hair tangled as seaweed flecked with salt, her lashes and the back of her coat weighed down with snow, her grey eyes as empty as the snow-laden sky was that day.

'I don't want to go to Aberdeen,' she said to him as he lifted her. 'I don't want to go to Aberdeen.'

Tormod's Journals

January 1919

It was that evening – once we'd got Rachel back to the safety and warmth of the house – that my grandfather began to talk about an event he sometimes wrote about in his journals: the sinking of the *Iolaire*. Nearly eighteen years of silence giving way after the events of the preceding few months. It was as if his walk down to the snow-covered shore in search of his grandaughter had, finally, put an end to his numbness, the ways in which he had tried to avoid speaking about all that happened in the early hours of January 1st, 1919.

In the journals, he sketched scenes from that night in a feverish way, showing the blurred outline of the ship, the smoky sheen of water as it went down that cold and drizzly night, the men on board in their uniforms, the sea quaking with a frenzy he had rarely seen troubling its surface before. In the darkness, too, Commander Mason – or, perhaps, another officer, Lieutenant Cotter – standing on deck. Quarrelling with others who claimed the ship had taken a wrong direction, an incorrect turn in its course. Their fingers pointing, the men declaring that the vessel was about to be wrecked near the shoreline. They prodded and jabbed their hands to justify this, mentioning again and again their knowledge of this port.

'We're used to this place. We've fished here for years.'

The Naval Officer was magnificent in his defiance of them. His chest broadened, his jaw jutted in anger, shouting loudly, his hand clenched into a fist.

'Do you think I don't know these waters? Have no idea of my trade…?'

'Well, if you're forcing us to say that…'

'That's just sheer bloody insolence! Who the hell do you think you are?'

Their quarrel was interrupted by a loud screeching noise, metal grinding against stone. It shuddered across the boat, tipping it to starboard. It was this moment that my grandfather wrote about succinctly, how he saw men fall off the side of the ship, heard their screams as another wave crashed into the vessel, pitching her further onto the rocks. He noted that some decided at this point to jump, even though they didn't have a clue where they were or which direction they should swim, one even trying to grab at Tormod and pull him by the sleeve to the *Iolaire*'s side. But Tormod shook him off and stood still, frozen where he was – his only movement was to slip that little oilcloth package with its drawings and jewellery inside his vest, next to his chest. He tried to work out where he was in the darkness. Where the ship lay in that harbour. How far out it was. How close it might be to the coastline of Lewis. Suddenly, a couple of flares went off, allowing him to see with a startling intensity for a moment. It was one of the fishermen who pointed out the ship wasn't that far from a ledge which stretched out from the shore.

'We can bloody do it!' someone shouted out. 'Land's only a wee bit away.'

Tormod saw more men dropping from the side of the ship. A rope around their waists, some perched for a moment on the railing, like birds about to leap into the waters to harvest fish. A few kneeled on the deck before diving, praying that God might somehow reach out a hand to save them. Like most of the other islanders on board, they were unable to swim, the sea with its currents swirling around their homes being regarded as much too cold and dangerous for them to enter for much of the year. They all trembled as they plunged, their Naval collars and bell bottom trousers flapping in the turbulence of the wind, their bodies flung this way and that by the forces of the blackness all around them. Perhaps their fear shook them too. Uncertainty and nerves. Some stayed silent as they jumped into the ocean, fists bunched and lips pressed tightly together. They might have been the ones who had done this before, hurtling into the Mediterranean or the North Atlantic when a U-boat or German battleship sank their vessel. They did it as if they were taking part in an absurd dance, their bodies jigging and jerking as they sprang from the deck. There were others to whom it all seemed much more of a surprise. Their eyes and mouths were open and distorted, shouting and screaming as they leaped, their yells muffled and silenced by the uproar of the waves.

I didn't want to listen to them, Tormod wrote. *I knew too many had died.*

The few lifeboats that were launched from the *Iolaire* didn't last long. One even shattered as they hitched it downward; its wood breaking and splintering as it struck the moving, heaving ship. There were mistakes and errors made, panic among those on board. Some of the men were not sure which direction they should take towards the shoreline, their minds and attention swirled as much by their own confusion as the fury of the seas. Waves breached and toppled them; two lifeboats floundered a short distance away from the ship. On another, Tormod saw a man whom he recognised vaguely in the darkness – John Finlay Macleod – jumping into the water, throwing his boots away first. They spun into the distance as he tied a leaving line about his wrist and tight within his grip. Light and thin, it was the line normally used to tug a heavier rope across from ship to shore. He slipped into the water clutching this, moving with a steady deliberation that most others lacked. Tormod saw all this in the blaze of another flare. Having learned to swim near his home, there was a purpose and intent to each sweep of John Finlay's arms, each kick and flurry of his legs. Land was only a short gasp away and he was determined to reach it, step once more onto its certainty and stillness.

And then there were those who were going in the opposite direction. Behind him on the vessel, Tormod was aware that there were some of the men climbing, scrambling up the masts of the *Iolaire* to cling like pigeons on trees that had shadowed them on the mainland, gulls and gannets on a pillar or skerry of stone. They hung there in small clusters, trusting that neither gravity nor surge would dislodge them. Already, he had seen one of them falling, a black-garbed being tumbling to the deck.

'Scream,' he heard himself say. 'Scream.'

That sound would be a sign that, for all that the pain was terrible, there might be life after the thud of landing on the lower level of the deck. There was none, however, just the man's trouser leg twitching in the wind, his back broken after his sudden fall. Tormod watched one of the other men go to see if the fallen figure, perhaps a friend of his, was still alive. A glimpse was all it took. A sad shake of the head confirming he was gone.

For a moment, Tormod wondered if he might go and join these men, hoping he could hold onto a mast till this nightmare was at an end and vessels came out from the harbour to save them. For someone like him, unable to swim, it seemed a safer choice than taking to the waves. He had a head for heights, he reasoned to himself, none for water or darkness. Besides, one look at the frenzy of the men who were taking to the sea was almost enough to persuade him to clamber upwards. Some of them were now racing fore and back, jerked sideways towards the ship's hull or metal railing, so much so that it looked as if a form of madness had taken hold of them, some fever had gripped both mind and body.

The explosion in the boiler convinced Tormod otherwise. He saw burning men running from its flames towards the side of the ship, plunging into the waves. He was aware, too, of more falling from their places upon the mast, shaken from where they roosted by the blast of flame and fire. Some screamed for their mothers; others for God or the arrival of angels among the waves. He knew that he was coming to that moment where he must make up his mind where to go. Stillness was no longer an option. He had stopped and watched long enough as the deck buckled and twisted below, distorted by the weight of water, the relentless heat. He ran to the side, suddenly seeing there was a rope fastened there just along the railing, a group of men standing around its knot.

'I think that someone's made it to the shore.'

'One of the fellows off the boat.'

'The rope's tight. Taut.'

'Hell...'

Finally, Tormod walked towards that gathering of men, trying to do so as calmly and slowly as he could. There were too many racing around in a panic, running back and fore as one thought after another stormed into their minds. A few moments later, he joined the group, conscious that Macdermid was just before him, aware that some other person he knew – Iain Help from the village – was a short distance away, a little ahead of him in this unearthly queue. Tormod didn't speak as he stood there, conscious that if he opened his mouth, a scream might give his fear away. He gritted his teeth together to prevent his terror breaking loose, to stop the pain and fright he felt from flooding outwards like the ocean, all the waves that rushed around his feet.

It was afterwards he made sense of it, how John Finlay Macleod had saved many of the lives of the men on board. He was the one who dived from the lifeboat, a line around his wrist, believing that the ledge of land was not far away, for all that the waves possessed the weight of boulders and he had nothing but hands and arms to shift them away, drawing himself through their rubble. There were rocks too, churning in the water, debris and obstacles on his way to shore. He felt them cut through his skin – the scythe-sharp waves, the edges of stone, the whiplash of each breaker. The chill of the water, too, bruised him. He felt each surge scoring against him all the way to his bones, taking him onwards, beyond where any man wished to go. Suddenly, though, he was on solid rock, gripping onto handholds he could barely see in the darkness, cracks and fissures in stone. Seconds later and he was almost washed back into the sea again. He climbed another yard upon the ledge, feeling the line tightening as he did so. This seemed to be about as far as he was able to go. He tugged and felt it escape from whatever had fastened it tight and hard; snared, perhaps, on an edge of rock or steel. The sudden movement gave him an extra yard or two, enough to stand firm without the risk of piling helter-skelter into the sea again.

'*Trobhad… Trobhad … Tha mi ann an seo!*' he yelled into the dark, hoping someone on board the *Iolaire* would hear him.

Some noise – like an echo – answered back.

And then something like a weight pulled on the heaving line. He could feel it like a heartbeat pulsing through the line, hand over hand, like the footsteps of a cat in the beginning but becoming closer and heavier as time went on, that weight becoming more solid as it emerged from the sea. Out of the turmoil of the waves, he began to recognise the outline of a man. Another fellow from Ness, Iain Help, coming over towards him.

'*Thàinig Iain!*' he yelled into the wind. 'Iain's arrived!'

There were others after that, straining on that rope, hauling themselves by their hands across the narrow channel between ship and shore. There were moments when John Finlay nearly toppled from the ledge, inches from falling into the sea. He was aware, too, that the rope might at any moment fray and break; it jerked from side to side as the ship moved, creaking when the bow ground against rock below the water's surface. The *Iolaire* would not stay upright for long. He was conscious that when it fell, it would mean an end to those trying to escape from the ship. Those whose lives were carried by the rope would also be cast into the waves. Already men were falling, their grip slipping due to either an instant of weakness or the wetness of the line they clutched. John Finlay would shout about this whenever breath and energy allowed him, yelling into the darkness.

'We need a hawser! A hawser!'

One of the Harrismen heard him, going with Tormod around the deck to find one that might suit.

'It's a bit short,' Tormod said, grimacing.

'Aye. And too thick to knot. But it'll have to do. We'll tie it to the other one.'

Hands numb and chilled, he helped fasten it. A tight knot. The bow knot… The cat's paw… Gripping sailor's hitch… He couldn't recall which one he used, but his fingers somehow possessed the knowledge. He tested the knot with all his strength, stretching it between his fingers. A moment later and he was leaving the sinking ship, shifting his fingers inch by inch, moving toward land. He was aware that Macdermid was in front of him, the two men shadowing each other as they had done for much of the last few years.

'Scream,' he kept saying to himself. 'Scream…'

He held the sound in until he grasped Macdermid's hand, the Harrisman having reached the shore just moments before him. He stretched out to clutch him, that grip helping to keep him upright. Prayerful hands. Holy fingers. Blessed by God. A tight clench of love and grace.

'You're safe, Tormod. You're safe.'

The scream ripped loose from him then, like a deep and deadly wound that had been sealed shut for a long time, rancid and poisonous. He hammered a rock with his fist and barely felt the pain. Some of the other men looked at him with surprise. John Finlay was resting, breathless and exhausted from all his exertions, but he managed to open an eye in his direction.

'You'd better help the others. Someone will need a rest.'

Tormod sat on the ground with Macdermid lodged behind him, the two men working together in a way they had never managed to do at sea, tugging hard at the rope. Other men were coming to shore now, their speed quickening, conscious that the vessel did not have much time left. Soon it would break and sink under the force of waves. Out of the edge of his gaze, he could see some of the survivors gathering together to raise the alarm, going to find people to help them rescue those who were still on the boat.

'Holm Farm isn't far away,' he heard someone say. 'We'd better go there, get help.'

He was dimly aware, too, that other survivors were not behaving in a rational way. One tried to drown out the endless screeching of both men and boat by singing the words of a Gaelic song, one that he had heard a short time before on the boat.

'*Eilean Fraoich, Eilean Fraoich,*
Eilean Fraoich nam beann àrd,
Far an d' fhuair mi m' àrach òg,
Eilean Leòdhais mo ghràidh.'

'*Heather isle, Heather isle,*

Heather isle of the high hills,
Where I was brought up in my youth,
Isle of Lewis that I love.'

Another was singing Psalm 23, and yet one more rushed around trying to find his brother, tapping men on their shoulders. '*Am faca sibh Murchadh? Am faca sibh Murchadh?* Have you seen Murdo? Have you seen Murdo?' An instant later, he was in the water again, looking desperately for the lad, some six years younger than himself, swimming out towards the boat to find him, never to be seen again. Shortly afterwards, another man did this, jumping into the sea while looking for a member of his family. And nearby, a survivor was praying, babbling aloud as he asked God what cruel trick was in His mind when He allowed these men to die a short distance from their homes.

'Why, Lord? Why this after these long years away? Why did You let this happen? We thought that You had brought peace to us.'

And then there were other hazards. The sheer size of the hawser proved a danger. Some men had hands that were too small to gain a decent grip; others were too clumsy to hold it tightly. The knot that Tormod had tied proved in itself an obstacle. Fingers slipped occasionally when men encountered it, defeated by its bulk and the greasiness of its surface. Some managed to hold on, trying not to be aware of the others tumbling into the sea that churned below them.

'Oh God, oh God, oh God… Why are you allowing this to happen just upon our shores? After all these years of war, what a trick to play on us!'

Tormod barely looked up, doing his best not to react to these faces as they fell from view. Even if they were familiar to him, even if he had sketched their faces only a short time before, it was better to pretend that he did not know who they were. Instead, he tried to keep the rope as straight and rigid as he could, for all that everything was conspiring around him – the wind, waves, the constant jagged rhythm of the boat as it lay trapped on the rocks – to prevent him and the others doing this. It danced and swayed, jerked up and down, lurched and jolted each time the vessel creaked and groaned. Once or twice he saw a man fall because of a movement he and the rest of them on shore had failed to control.

'Scream,' he said once again, willing them not to remain silent, to die with some sound on their lips. 'Scream. Scream. Scream.'

And then the vessel became cracked and broken, the rope slackened, and there seemed no point in holding onto it anymore.

1937

The days when he hitched up the mare to the gig, Grandad remembered what it had been like in Stornoway that New Year's Day back in 1919.

There had been so many carts trundling through the town during that time, rattling through its streets to and from the Battery where ammunition had been cleared from the largest room and a makeshift mortuary created. Their only loads were the corpses fished out of the harbour; those strewn around the Beasts of Holm or washed up elsewhere – at the foot of someone's croft, perhaps, near the Airnish lighthouse, even swirling in the direction of the pier. Each one was wrapped up in tarpaulin to prevent people seeing what lay within: damaged bodies, scarred faces, bruised and broken skin, bones jutting outwards from men's flesh. Not that any of it mattered. Anyone looking on already knew what they contained. Tears flecked their cheeks as they imagined the features of those they loved and cared for, lost to them from that moment onwards. They knew that their husbands and fathers could have been on the *Iolaire*. The telegrams they carried within their fingers, used occasionally to wipe their faces, gave them the news that they were likely to have travelled on the ship.

Leaving soon on Iolaire STOP See you soon
STOP

Both Iolaire and Sheila sailing STOP
Hoping to sail on the first faster ship
STOP See you tomorrow STOP

Tormod had tried not to think about it. Even though he
was aware that these corpses were being stretched out on
tables in the Battery, some with a note attached indicating
the villages from which they came, something decided after
their pockets had been scoured and searched for letters they
had received, identity discs that hung around their necks.
Shawbost, Carloway, Uig, Ness – a litany of place names,
some, perhaps, his neighbours in South Dell. Even though
there were already relatives weeping over these bodies,
mourning a dead son or husband whom only a few hours
before – when they had tucked themselves up in bed – they
had expected to come home either in the morning or during
the hours of darkness, interrupting their dreams. Instead,
Tormod had walked through the streets of Stornoway that
January 1st, passing the shops and offices: Charles Morrison,
Mackenzie and MacFarlane (General Merchants), the
British Linen Bank, the 'English' kirk, the black and scorched
walls of the old Town Hall, which had burned down a few
months before. He found himself looking through windows,
examining the structure of walls, even the pattern of the soot
staining the stone of the skeleton of that building, grateful
for every sight that might divert him, glad too that there
was a cold wind numbing him, one that froze and chilled
the very stuff of bones. He continued to feel that way even

when he heard that Am Patch had been saved, clinging on until daylight to the mast while all the others, both above and below him, had dropped off. What did it matter that one of the *Iolaire*'s passengers had finally stepped onto the pier when he arrived in Stornoway, just like all the others had been supposed to do all those hours before? Wasn't that just God playing one of His awful jokes?

It wasn't the only way he had diverted himself. When the carts rattled past, instead of glancing upwards at their cargo of the dead, he looked down at their wheels, noting how well their felloes had been made and shaped, examining the state and condition of their spokes, recalling too the tools that were involved in the making of them – the tyre dog, tampers, sledge-hammer, roller – waiting for him in the yard when he reached South Dell. Regardless of this day, he would soon have to pick them up again, especially now that Calum was crippled. It would be Tormod's task to fasten the blacksmith's apron, raise a hammer to the anvil, no longer Calum's. He laughed at this thought, making the tears of some passer-by cease or falter for an instant, before he began to pay the same kind of close attention to the horses that clipped and galloped along the road. He found himself analysing the state of repair of their shoes, how neatly their manes and tails had been brushed, their withers, hindquarters, hooves; looking too at the way that horse and cart were hitched together, just like those men – probably dead now – who had got down on their knees at Kyle of Lochalsh railway station, examining the manner in which the railwaymen coupled engine and coach, as if they were planning to acquire skills that would help them engineer their own trains, one that might run from Stornoway to Carloway, all the way to Ness. He recalled, too, the words he had learned for 'horse' in his travels and repeated them, using them to drum the thought of all these shadows from his head.

'Each. Equus. Capall. Ceffyl. Cheval. Pferd. Caballo.'

And, ever since that first day of January in 1919, all this was in his mind each time he fixed his gig to get ready to go to Stornoway, every time he travelled along that road Leverhulme's money had helped to create, past villages like Galson, Borve, Shader and Barvas. He knew that these places all had their homes to which the men from the *Iolaire* had once belonged. Some of the more than two hundred who had been killed. Or even the seventy or so who had been saved, slipping from the wreckage just before the vessel had gone down not far from the harbour, brought to shore by hawser and rope, the strength and efforts of John Finlay Macleod swimming from the Beasts of Holm. And then there were the houses which he could identify as having lost their sons for other reasons, emigrating to Canada because they could no longer bear the bleakness of the place, that sense of loss and mourning that so many of the women showed in their dark clothing, so many of the men hid deep within their souls, unable to let slip a word of how they felt.

And it was all being made worse by the words of Alvar Lidell whispering from the Revophone Crystal Set the headmaster brought every few days into school. He spoke of the fighting that was in Spain, the pacts and agreements between Hitler and Mussolini, Germany and Japan, the men condemned to death in trials that were taking place in

Moscow. I was the one who relayed all this, never noticing how Grandad's face darkened each time these matters were mentioned, how Grandma forgot to thank God for the coming of the wireless in her prayers, how Calum shook his head as he hobbled around the house on a pair of walking sticks.

'The whole thing's coming round again,' he muttered. 'It's as if we're living upon a wheel. As if the whole Earth is felloed with madness and death.'

But I was aware of little of that. Dad had sent me Alan Breck's *Book of Scottish Football* and I had it on my lap as we travelled along, leafing through its pages as we made our way through the villages, looking at the photographs of players, dreaming of Willie Mills and Matt Armstrong, reading an account of the Scotland football team touring North America. And all the time, too, I was asking questions that my grandad could not possibly have answered.

'Is Jimmy Delaney as good as they say he is? He scored two goals against Germany.'

'What do you think of Bob McPhail?'

'Do you think we'll beat Rangers for the league this year?'

'Will Dad take me to watch Scotland play at Hampden?'

'I suppose he'll do his best,' Grandad grunted as we began to make our way across the moor. This time, though, its emptiness did not appal me. I took note of the occasional sheep I saw upon it, as if I was planning to report back the presence of some flock or other to my great-uncle. I watched, too, the men who stayed in Barvas Lodge. They stood in the shallows of the river that runs across much of the moor, rods in their hands. In the glitter of that water, they cast the only shadows apart from a heron that stood near the bank, still and impenetrable. Nearby some sheep grazed, their fleeces a murky white in the brown shades of moor.

'Draw that,' Grandad said to me. 'Keep it in your head for all time. Together with all the birds you saw last summer. Remember how they flapped and flew. You never know when you might need some of that spirit inside you. Make sure you find it there.'

'I'll do that.'

'Promise me.'

'I will.'

Grandad drove the gig steadily along the road, stopping occasionally to give way to a lorry, a van bringing stock to one of the local shops, an Austin 7 saloon steered in the direction of some emergency by a doctor travelling either north or to the island's west side. We went past, too, the occasional loch or peatstack, a flurry of lapwings, a curlew with its tearful cries, making our way to Newmarket and Laxdale on the edge of town.

'Nearly there now. Nearly there.'

It was as if the fact that he said this shook him. His body quivered as we travelled along Cromwell Street, seeing the shops again – Charles Morrison, Mackenzie and MacFarlane (General Merchants), the British Linen Bank – before turning to the pier where the *Lochness* was waiting, its gangway in place, ready to take its passengers across to Mallaig and Kyle of Lochalsh.

1992

We never saw them again after that, just their words in the rare letters they would send to our new home in Aberdeen. Rachel and I became citizens of that place, becoming part of all the locations in the city – from the Winter Gardens to the beach, Duthie Park to Torry – that my father had mentioned when he'd occasionally written to us. There were days when, just as Dad had predicted, we became familiar with the taste of ice cream in our mouths, the warm wrap of gold and black scarves around our throats, the names of football players like Willie Mills and Matt Armstrong, the words of songs they sang at half-time, verses of 'Loch Lomond', the songs of Harry Lauder, 'Keep Right On To The End Of The Road', 'Roamin' In The Gloamin'', each one bellowed out as loudly as voice and spirit could allow.

There were other things we could never have foreseen: how our father lurched – all too often – from drink to drink as he stumbled from bar to bar the length and breadth of Union Street; how he switched, too, from job to job, never holding down steady work on either quayside or factory while he lived there; how there would be nights when he would sit in our home in Aberdeen, nursing a cloud of cigarettes and a half bottle of whisky and talking of returning to the shipyards on the Clyde where he had been employed before.

'Ah tell ye, George Cruickshank has nae lack i' freens in Glescae. Nae doot aboot 'at. If Ah gid back aire, aire'd be fowk aroon tae help me cope an' support me. Ah can rest assured aboot 'at.'

Neither could we predict that the moment would soon come when his own family would turn upon him again, when I would arrive at his brother or sister's door to hear them turn round and declare, 'No. We dinna want any of Geordie Cruickshank's bairns roon here. Just in case they turn out to ha'e sticky fingers like their faither. If he cam roond here, I widnae trust him wae his haun on the door-knob. Or the letter boax.'

And that is why I look back at my life with my grandparents as the greatest days in my young life. They provided me with a sense of decency, this ability to sketch and draw and see the world in both its full horrors and delights, which – for many years of my life – helped me earn a living.

Yet there is more than that. I am reminded of my grandfather every time I see so many wonders in my life, such as the birds he told me I had to notice, the heron we saw on that last journey together, still and stalwart, standing upright through the storms that so often scurried across that island; their presence providing me, in the lift of wings, the lilt of song, the lights and shadow of their plumage, a wonder-strewn example of how a man can live out his days.

He has the right to sing too.

He also has to find his own way to fly.

AGC
August 1992

Author's note

My home village of South Dell was not one of those most affected by the *Iolaire* disaster. Scroll through the names of those whose lives were ended by the tragedy that took place on January 1st, 1919 on the edge of Stornoway harbour and you will find the name of only one individual from the village among the dead: Angus Gillies of 35 South Dell. Balancing this, there was only one man too from that small community among the survivors: Iain Help (or John Murray) of 6a South Dell. As he was married and living in the village of Back, it is two of his five brothers – Dòdubh (or Donald) and Tòhan (or Norman) – that I recall. Both lived in the village, with the latter being particularly memorable. He had spent years in Montana, that time marked by his distinctive choice of headgear. There weren't many men who wore a Stetson in the South Dell of my youth.

Together with my own grandfather, Dòmhnall Stufain (or Donald Murray), who served in the Dardanelles (or Gallipoli) campaign, Iain Help is among the few 'real' people mentioned in *As The Women Lay Dreaming*. Aside from an occasional glimpse of my family and neighbours, most who fall into that category come from the other end of the parish, specifically John Finlay Macleod from Port of Ness, whose bravery and courage saved the majority of those who survived the tragedy, swimming to shore with a rope tied to his wrist. And Am Patch (or Donald Morrison) from Knockaird, heroic in another sense, clinging to the mast of the sinking vessel till daylight and rescue arrived; managing to hold on even as many fell from their positions around him, their grip slipping and failing in the penetrating cold of that midwinter night. This was despite the way that many had fallen from their positions around him, their grip slipping and failing in the penetrating cold of that midwinter night. In many ways, his rescue was an unexpected postscript to a tragedy that had its effect on the Gaelic-speaking, crofting townships of Lewis for decades; its effect palpable even in the sixties and seventies when I was growing up in the district of Ness.[1]

I recall both these men from my youth. I saw Am Patch – who died in 1990 at the age of ninety-two – fairly often, pacing the village road, perhaps heading to the shop at the crossroads in Lionel, which was, for many years, the focus of the northern tip of Ness in Lewis. My recollection of John Finlay Macleod – who passed away in 1978 – is also strong, largely prompted by the hushed voice of my Uncle Norman, a figure mentioned briefly in these pages. He took

---

[1] There seems to me to be a difference between the way the town of Stornoway and the rural districts of the island experienced the *Iolaire* disaster. There is no doubt that the impact on the town was both more immediate and dramatic – the people seeing the corpses being carted through its streets. However, the effect on country districts was both long-term and sustained, with several villages – such as North Tolsta, Bragar, Shawbost and those in the parish of Uig – losing a considerable number of their young men.

me to the boatyard in Port of Ness where that particular survivor of the *Iolaire* worked for many years. 'He's a hero, the one who saved so many,' Norman whispered, before ushering me through the door to see a man who, with his slender build, cloth cap and dungarees, seemed a slight and insubstantial figure for the role both history and Norman had thrust upon him. As a child, I expected heroes to step with the swagger and sway of my favourite cowboy, John Wayne. Nowadays I am glad they rarely do, that they are most often ordinary, modest and gentle individuals, chosen sometimes by fate or chance or God. Even recalling his placid, unruffled demeanour that day does a little to restore my faith in humanity, battered as it has been by the politics of the last few years.

There are other parts of the story that are true. The ship's officers on the fateful voyage of the *Iolaire*, Mason and Cotter, also appear in the novel with the biographical details of the former being substantially correct. This is also the case with several of the naval battles mentioned. Sometimes I keep to the literal facts, as in the account of the Battle of Jutland, which I have drawn from several sources. I also, however, switch details from one naval skirmish or sinking and transfer it to another, largely using the voices of those involved in the war at sea during this period. Some of the boats I mention – like the *Glengarry*, which was in reality a mailboat on Loch Ness – are fictional; others are genuine. I trust that this approach is both understandable and defensible. Unlike the soldiers involved in trench warfare on the Western Front during the conflict, there are few recorded accounts of those involved in the First World

War at sea. They include books like Nigel Steel and Peter Hart's *Jutland, 1916: Death In The Grey Wastes* (Cassell 2003), Robert K Massie's *Castles of Steel* (Vintage, 2007), Robert C Stern's *Battle Beneath The Waves* (Arms and Armour, 1999) and Max Arthur's *Forgotten Voices Of The Great War* (Ebury Press, 2002). (I also wanted to provide a sense of the scale of the war at sea – from the North Sea to the South Atlantic, from the Gallipoli campaign to the Falklands.) Though their ends were every bit as cruel – and much more certain – than their counterparts on land, their voices are muted and rarely heard by our contemporaries. There is an imbalance in the way the Great War has been recorded, with those from the periphery – such as those who signed up for the Royal Naval Reserve from islands like the Western Isles, Shetland and Orkney – often ignored in our historical reckonings of that period. There are all sorts of reasons for this. They include not just the geographical position of those who took part but also language and class. These men rarely spoke – far less wrote – of their years at sea or war. They put up with and shut up about all they had suffered. When they broke that bond of silence, however, as in '*An Eala Bhàn*' ('The White Swan'), the song written by Dòmhnall Ruadh Chorùna (or Donald MacDonald) from North Uist, the results are both fine and moving, revealing a tenderness and poignancy that is seldom matched by even the great poets who chronicled the First World War in English.

The people of both Lewis and the islands as a whole largely reacted with a restrained and mute dignity to all that they experienced during their years at war and the immediate

aftermath.[2] They suffered the highest losses of any part of
the British Isles during the conflict; the extent of the fatalities
summed up by the day in May 1915 that I mention in the
novel, when there were no less than nine deaths reported to
those who resided in the parish. This led to many households
in South Dell being occupied by single women, either unmar-
ried or widowed, the only clothes hanging in their wardrobes
a uniform and unrelenting shade of black. They wore this
outfit day in, day out for decades. Sometimes their brothers
stayed with them. In their different ways, both genders were
trapped by the absence of men; not only the dead but also
those sent into exile by the dire economic situation of the
Western Isles following the war. For women who wished
to take the traditional route of marriage and children, there
were few men around with whom they could share their
lives. Even for these males, however, the situation possessed
more than its share of difficulties. Marriage might mean they
would have to evict sisters from their childhood homes. Or
it could also mean an intimacy of which they were no longer
capable, a wall, perhaps, built around them by their years
of war. (There was one man I recall – and allude to in the
novel – who suffered severe psychological damage through
the loss of his three brothers, a couple of incidents, too,
where the vessel on which he served had gone down at sea.
He greeted each morning by brandishing a walking stick in

---

[2] One could argue that this attitude had its own problems, as I try to show
in the novel. There is a negative side to forbearance. Lips can be buttoned
too long; views and opinions left unexpressed. We should be very careful
about idealising the passivity of the past. It created its own difficulties for
those who lived through it.

his hand, unleashing loud shouts and cries on the growing light of day – for all that I have no clear memory of what he said.) Far better in these circumstances to switch off that part of yourself that ached for love, tenderness, sex. There is little doubt in my mind that this, too, had its own harmful effect on people. The heart (often) needs a home and people (sometimes) ache and hurt when they fail to find one.

There are other truthful aspects to this story. Sometimes these involve my own family history. As I write in my book *The Dark Stuff* (Bloomsbury, 2018), my Great-Uncle Allan was paralysed down one side of his body as a result of an illness contracted in Liverpool around the beginning of the First World War. Like Calum in *As The Women Lay Dreaming*, he was often to be found wandering the Ness moor, helping others to look after their sheep. My maternal grandmother also died in Glasgow when she was still a young woman, leaving her husband and three children to cope on their own. As a result, my mother and her brother, Archie, lived for a time together with her grandmother – my great-grandmother – on the island of Tiree. Like the characters in this book, this was a time of healing for her after a traumatic period in her life. After this, however, truth and fiction part company. Their father worked in the Merchant Navy, not the shipyards alongside the Clyde. He was from Skye and not Aberdeen. Neither – it should be pointed out – was he a habitual thief.

My great-great-grandparents were both married twice in similar circumstances to the fictional Tormod and Catriona Morrison, but there are no equivalents either to them or their family in real life. There was also never a blacksmith at that address in South Dell. Come to think of it... There is not even that specific address – 16b – in South Dell, though I had a particular ruined building in mind when I wrote this book (it sat in the corner of a neighbour's croft). Some of my legends about the landscape of the village are also utterly fanciful, though this is not the case with them all. I leave it to the reader to find out which ones were genuine parts of village folklore and which were decidedly not.

In short, this book is a novel and as such an imaginative creation – though one that relies for its inspiration on the real landscape of both South Dell and Ness generally. Despite this, I owe a tremendous debt to the works on which I have drawn, most especially John Macleod's powerful *When I Heard The Bell* (Birlinn, 2010) and the magnificent *The Going Down Of The Sun – Dol Fodha na Grèine*, the creation of Comunn Eachdraidh Nis (Ness Historical Society) and published by Acair in 2014. Some of the fictional works that have helped to generate this work include: *War and Turpentine* (Vintage, 2016) by the Dutch writer Stefan Hertmans; *To Die In Spring* (Picador, 2017) by the German writer Ralf Rothmann; and *All Quiet On The Western Front* (Vintage, 1996) by Erich Maria Remarque. The descriptions of early twentieth-century Newfoundland in the book owe a little to the work of Wayne Johnston, particularly *Baltimore's Mansion* (Anchor Books, 2000) and *The Colony of Unrequited Dreams* (Anchor Books, 1999). I also drew inspiration from the writings of John Dos Passos and some of the imagery found in the poem 'Mappa Mundi' by David Constantine (*Collected Poems*, Bloodaxe, 1991). One night, for the people of the isle of Lewis, Charon did arrive in a dark ship.

I owe a historical debt, too, to both Calum Ferguson, of Point and Stornoway, and the late Norman Malcolm Macdonald, of Tong, whose Gaelic book *Call na H-Iolaire* (Acair, 2003) began to open the historical silence that affected Lewis society in relation to the *Iolaire* tragedy for many years. One individual – the chair of Stornoway Historical Society, Malcolm Macdonald (whose name closely resembles that of Tormod/Norman) – also added considerably to our awareness of the events of that morning in 1919. When I visited Eyemouth a number of years ago, someone suggested that it had taken that township around a century to begin to get over its own tragedy in 1881 – when 189 fishermen, most part of that community, were drowned. A hundred years have now passed since the sinking of the *Iolaire*. Let what healing that has occurred over recent years continue.

I have also been delighted – over the past twelve or so years since I started working on this book – to have received the assistance of a large number of people, too many to name here. I must, however, give an especial thanks to a few individuals who looked at the manuscript at various points in its creation. These include my friends Doug Robertson, Drew Ratter (who helped by pointing me towards some of the naval battles of World War One), Donald Anderson, Tom Clark, Mairianna Mackenzie, Donald MacSween, Cathy Macdonald, Ian MacDonald, Iain Gordon Macdonald, Matthew MacIver, Donald 'Ryno' Morrison, Chris Nicolson, James Sinclair and others. (A number of these people have been there for me at various points in my life.) There were others who assisted in other ways, including Les Sinclair for his assistance with Doric, and Chris Gavin who is the official historian for Aberdeen FC. My son, Angus Murray, also took me for a strenuous walk in Skye which assisted me – whether he was aware of this or not – in the making of this book. This is also true of – among many others – my daughter, Eileen, and brother, Allan. I would also like to thank the staff of various museums and libraries. These include the Archives Department of Shetland Museum and Communn Eachdraidh Nis, as well as those of Stornoway and Shetland Libraries. The latter has played host to me on many occasions in the past few years. The staff have always made me more than welcome.

I want to specifically thank too Sara Hunt for her faith and support in publishing this novel as well as Craig Hillsley for his hard work in helping to shape the book. He performed miracles in doing so! I am very grateful too to Angus Campbell for his consent in allowing me to use a short extract from his great-uncle Murdo MacFarlane's song about the *Iolaire*, and I'm delighted that Niall O'Gallagher has given me permission to use his translation of the work. (I recall Murdo walking down the street in Stornoway and my fellow villager, Dòmhnall Ban, telling me there hadn't been his likes in Scotland since Robert Burns. In terms of his music and general creativity, there wasn't much of an exaggeration going on there.) Another individual whom I would like to thank for his creativity is Andrew Forteath. His skill and artistry was responsible for designing the wonderful cover of this book. Thanks are also due to Paola Cardenas for the maps and family tree and to Madeleine Pollard for her editorial assistance.

Finally, I want to dedicate this book to two people, my wife, Maggie Priest – for her continual love, support and patience – and my late friend Alex Cluness, who passed away earlier this year. Among his many acts of kindness towards me was his suggestion that the book need a short opening section set in Glasgow to 'work'. In this, and so much else, he was right. The people of Ness, Lewis – and South Dell specifically – have also provided a different form of inspiration for me, both in art and life. It is only right in these final words to acknowledge this and give thanks to them.

Donald S Murray
June 2018

From *The Stornoway Gazette,*
5 January, 1919

No one now alive in Lewis can ever forget the 1st January 1919, and future generations will speak of it as the blackest day in the history of the island, for on it 200 of our bravest and best perished on the very threshold of their homes under the most tragic circumstances. The terrible disaster at Holm on New Year's morning has plunged every house and every heart in Lewis into grief unutterable. Language cannot express the anguish, the desolation, the despair which this awful catastrophe has inflicted. One thinks of the wide circle of blood relations affected by the loss of even one of the gallant lads, and imagination sees those circles multiplied by the number of the dead, overlapping and overlapping each other till the whole island – every hearth and home it is shrouded in deepest gloom.

From *The Scotsman*,
6 January, 1919

The appalling catastrophe at Stornoway still monopolises all thoughts on the island. The villages of Lewis are like places of the dead. No one goes about except on duties that cannot be left undone. The homes of the island are full of lamentation – grief that cannot be comforted. Carts in little processions of twos and threes, each bearing its coffin from the mortuary, pass through the streets of Stornoway on their way to some rural village, and all heads are bared as they pass. Scarcely a family has escaped the loss of some near blood relation. Many have had sorrow heaped on sorrow. Messages of sympathy and offers of what help is possible continue to pour in from all quarters.